Bjørnstjerne Bjørnson

Captain Mansana & Mothers Hands

Bjørnstjerne Bjørnson

Captain Mansana & Mothers Hands

ISBN/EAN: 9783337076665

Printed in Europe, USA, Canada, Australia, Japan

Cover: Foto ©Andreas Hilbeck / pixelio.de

More available books at **www.hansebooks.com**

CAPTAIN MANSANA

&

MOTHER'S HANDS

BY

BJÖRNSTJERNE BJÖRNSON

Translated from the Norwegian

LONDON
WILLIAM HEINEMANN
1897

BIBLIOGRAPHICAL NOTE.

[The two somewhat anomalous stories which are here published together have little in common except the difficulty of finding a place for them in the category of Björnson's works.

"Captain Mansana," under the title of "Kaptejn Mansana, en Fortælling fra Italien," was originally printed, in 1875, in the Norwegian periodical "Fra Fjeld og Dal." It did not appear in book form until August 1879, when it was published, in a paper cover with a startling illustration, in Copenhagen. "Captain Mansana" was written at Aulestad. It was almost immediately published in a Swedish, and later in a German, translation.

A Norwegian magazine, entitled "Nyt Tidsskrift," was started in Christiania in 1882, and continued to represent extreme liberal views in Norway until 1887, when it ceased to appear. In 1892 an attempt was made to resuscitate this periodical, under the general editorship of J. E. Sars. The first number of this new series appeared in November of that year, the opening article being the story of "Mors hænder" ("Mother's Hands"). It was reprinted in August 1894, in the collection called "Nye Fortællinger." It is now for the first time translated into English.

E. G.]

CAPTAIN MANSANA

AUTHOR'S PREFACE.

THE following note was prefixed by the author to the first edition of "Captain Mansana: an Italian Tale":

This story was originally published, several years ago, in a Danish Christmas Annual, "From Hill and Dale," which was edited by Mr. H. J. Greensteen. "Captain Mansana" has already run through two editions in German, and many friends have urged the author to republish it, in a separate form, and in his own tongue.

The following remarks seem necessary in consequence of some criticisms which have appeared in the Danish and Swedish press. The narrative, in all essential particulars, is based on facts, and those of its incidents which appear most extraordinary, are absolutely historical, the minutest details being in some cases reproduced. Mansana himself is drawn from life. The achievements credited to him in these pages, are those he actually performed ; and his singular experiences are here correctly described, so far, at least, as they bear upon his psychological development.

The causes which induced me to make him the subject of the following sketch may be found in a few lines of Theresa Leaney's letter, with which the story closes. The reader should compare Theresa's observations on Mansana, with the account of Lassalle, given contemporaneously with the original publication of this story, by Dr. Georg Brandes in his work on the "Nineteenth Century." Any one who studies the masterly portrait painted by Brandes, will observe that the inner forces which shaped Lassalle's destiny are precisely the same as those that swayed Mansana. No doubt Lassalle, with his fertile intellect, his commanding personality, and his inexhaustible energy, touches a far higher level of interest. Still, the phase of character is similar in the two cases, and it struck me at the time as curious, that both Dr. Brandes and myself should have had our attention simultaneously directed to it.

BJÖRNSTJERNE BJÖRNSON

CAPTAIN MANSANA

CHAPTER I

I was on my way to Rome, and as I entered the train at Bologna, I bought some newspapers to read on my journey. An item of news from the capital, published in one of the Florence journals, immediately arrested my attention. It carried me back thirteen years, and brought to mind a former visit I had paid to Rome, and certain friends with whom I had lived in a little town in the vicinity, at the time when Rome was still under the Papal rule.

The newspaper stated that the remains of the patriot Mansana had been exhumed from the Cemetery of the Malefactors in Rome, at the petition of the inhabitants of his native town, and that in the course of the next few days, they were to be received by the town council and escorted by deputations from various patriotic associations in Rome and the neighbouring cities to A——, Mansana's birthplace. A monument had been prepared there, and a ceremonial reception awaited the remains : the deeds of the martyred hero were at length to receive tardy acknowledgment.

It was in the house of this Mansana that I had lodged thirteen years before ; his wife and his younger brother's wife had been my hostesses. Of the two brothers themselves, one was at that time in prison in Rome, the other in exile in Genoa. The newspaper recapitulated the story of the elder Mansana's career. With all, except the latter portion, I was already pretty well acquainted, and for that reason I felt a special desire to accompany the procession, which was to start from the Barberini Palace in Rome the following Sunday, and finish its journey at A——.

On the Sunday, at seven o'clock in the morning of a grey October day, I was at the place of assembly. There was collected a large number of banners, escorted by the delegates, who had been selected by the various associations : six men, as a rule, from each. I took up my position near a banner that bore the legend :- " The Fight for the Fatherland," and amongst the group which surrounded it. They were men in red shirts, with a scarf round the body, a cloak over the shoulders, trousers thrust into high boots, and broad-leaved plumed hats. But what faces these were ! How instinct with purpose and determination ! Look at the well-known portrait of Orsini, the man who threw bombs at Napoleon III.; in him you have the typical Italian cast of countenance often seen in the men who had risen against the tyranny in Church and State, braving the dungeon and the scaffold, and had leagued themselves together in those formidable organisations from which sprang the army that liberated Italy. Louis Napoleon had himself been a member of one of these associations, and he had sworn, like all his comrades, that whatsoever position he might gain, he would use it to further Italy's unity and happiness, or in default that he would forfeit his own life. It was Orsini, his former comrade in the Carbonari, who reminded Napoleon of his oath, after he had become Emperor

3

of the French. And Orsini did it in the manner best calculated to make the Emperor realise the fate which awaited him if he failed to keep his pledge.

The first time I saw Orsini's portrait the idea flashed across my mind that ten thousand such men might conquer the world. And now, as I stood here, I had before me those whom the same feeling for their country's wrongs had animated with the same intense passion. Over that passion a kind of repose had fallen now, but the gloomy and lowering brows showed that it was not the tranquillity of content. The medals on their breasts proved that they had been present at Porta San Pancrazio in 1849 (when Garibaldi, though outnumbered by the French troops, twice forced them to retreat), in 1858, at the Lake of Garda, in 1859 in Sicily and Naples. And it was probable enough, though there were no medals to testify to *that* fact, that the history of their lives would have revealed their share in the day of Mentana. This is one of those battlefields which is not recognised by the Government, but which has burnt itself most deeply into the hearts of the people, as Louis Napoleon learnt to his cost. He had formally secured the help of Italy against the Germans in 1870 ; the remembrance of Mentana made it impossible for King and Government to carry out the agreement. It would have been as much as Victor Emmanuel's throne was worth to have done that.

The contrast between this dark and formidable determination of the Italians, and their mocking gaiety and reckless levity, is just as marked as that between the resolute countenances of the Orsini type, such as I noticed here, and the frivolous faces, which express nothing but a contemptuous superiority or mere indifference. Faces of this type were also to be seen among the spectators, or among the delegates who accompanied the banners inscribed " The Press," " Freethought," " Freedom for Labour," and so on. Involuntarily I thought, it is this element of frivolity among one half of the population that brings out a sterner element of resolution in the other half. The greater, the more general, this frivolity, the stronger and fiercer must be the passionate energy of those who would prevail against it. And through my brain there coursed reminis-

cences of the past history of Italy, with its contrasts of strange levity and dark purpose. Back-
ward and forward my thoughts swayed, from Brutus
to Orsini, from Catiline to Cæsar Borgia, from
Lucullus to Leo X., from Savonarola to Garibaldi.
Meanwhile the company got itself in motion, the
banners streamed out, loud-voiced street-vendors
offered for sale leaflets and pamphlets containing
accounts of Mansana's career, and the procession
passed into the Via Felice. Silence greeted it as
it moved on. The lofty houses showed few
spectators at this early hour, fewer still as the
procession turned into the Via Venti-Settembre,
past the Quirinal ; but the onlookers were somewhat more numerous as the party came down
into the Forum and passed out of the city by the
Colosseum to the Porta Giovanni. Outside the
gate the hearse, which had been provided by the
Municipality and driven by its servants, was in
waiting. This hearse was immediately set in
motion. Close behind it walked two young men,
one in civil costume, the other in the uniform of
an officer of the Bersaglieri. Both were tall,
spare, muscular, with small heads and low fore-
heads ; resembling one another in build and

6

features, and yet infinitely different. They were the sons of the dead Mansana.

I could recall them as boys of thirteen or fourteen, and the episode round which my recollection of them gathered was curious enough : I remembered their old grandmother throwing stones at these boys as they stood laughing, beyond her reach. I had a sudden distinct vision of the old woman's keen, angry eyes, of her sinewy, wrinkled hands, her grey bristling hair round her coffee-coloured face ; and now, as I looked at the boys, I could almost have said that the stones she threw had not missed their mark, and were deep in their hearts still.

How the grandmother had hated them ! Had they given her no special cause for this hatred ? Assuredly they had, for hate breeds hate, and strife strife. But how did it begin ? I was not with them at the time, but it was not difficult to understand the origin of it all.

She had been left a widow early in life, this old lady ; and all the interest and sympathy she gained by her comeliness and charm she tried to turn into a source of profit for herself and her two sons, the elder of whom was now lying here in his coffin. They were the only beings on earth she loved, and love them she did with a passionate frenzy of which the lads themselves eventually grew weary. Then, too, when they understood the species of cunning that lay in the use she made of her opportunities as a fascinating young widow, to gain material advantages for her sons, they began to feel a certain contempt for her. And so they turned from her, and threw all their energies into the ideas of Italian freedom and Italian unity which they had acquired from young and ardent companions. Their mother's narrow and frantic absorption in her own personal interests and affections made them only the more anxious to sacrifice everything for the common welfare.

In force of character, these boys not merely equalled their mother, but excelled her. Thus there arose a bitter struggle, in which in the end she succumbed.; but not until the young men's connections with the secret associations had procured for them a circle of acquaintance that extended far beyond the town and the society to which her family belonged. Each of them brought home a bride from a household of a higher social standing than their mother's, with a trousseau better than hers had been, and a dowry which, as she was bound to acknowledge, was respectable. This silenced her for awhile; it was clear that the business of playing the patriot had its advantages.

But the time came when both sons were forced to flee; when the elder was taken and imprisoned; when the most atrocious public extortion was practised; and when ruffianly officials regarded the defenceless widows as their prey. Their house had to be mortgaged, and then first one and then the other of their two vineyards; and finally one of their fields was seized by the mortgagees. And thus it came about that these ladies of gentle birth, friends from childhood, had to work like servants in the fields, the vineyard, and the house; they had to take lodgers, and wait on them; and worse than all this, to listen to words of insult and con-tumely, and that from others besides the clergy, who, under the Papal rule, were absolute masters in the town. For at that time few paid any tribute of respect to the wives of the men who had made sacrifices for their country, or, like

them, looked forward to the triumph of freedom, enlightenment, and justice. Now, indeed,
in the end the old woman had won! But
what did victory mean? Tears for her slighted
affection, her rejected counsels, her ruined property ; and she would rise and curse the sons
who had deceived and plundered her, till a
single glance from her elder daughter-in-law
drove her back to the chimney corner, where
she used to sit and pass her time in silent torpor,
while this mood was upon her. Then she would
sally out, and if she met her grandsons, in whom
she sorrowfully noticed the same keen glance
under the low brows, which she had first loved
and afterwards learned to fear in her own sons,
she would draw them to her with a torrent of
angry words. She would warn them against
their father's example, and inveigh against the
people, as a mere rabble, not worth the sacrifice
of a farthing, to say nothing of the loss of fortune, family, and freedom ; and she would rail
at her sons, the fathers of these boys, as the
handsomest, but most ungrateful and impractic-
able children whom any mother in the town had
brought to manhood. And pushing them angrily

from her, the unhappy woman would address the boys in accents of half-distracted appeal : " Do try and have more sense, you good-for-nothing scoundrels, you, instead of standing there and grinning at me. Don't be like those silly mothers of yours in there, who are bewitched by my sons' madness. But, God knows, there are mad folks on all sides of me." Then she would thrust the lads from her, weeping, and bury herself in her retreat. As time went on, neither she nor the boys stood on ceremony with one another. They laughed at her, when she was in one of her fits of despondency, and she threw stones at them ; and at last it came to this, that if they merely saw her sitting alone, they would call out, " Grandmamma, haven't you gone mad again ? " and then the expected volley of stones would follow.

But why did the old woman hardly dare to utter a syllable in the presence of her daughter-in-law ? For the same reason as that which had impelled her to keep silence before her sons in former times. Her own husband had been a man of delicate health, quite unequal to the strain of managing his worldly affairs ; he had married her in order that she might supply his deficiencies. She had undoubtedly increased the value of his property; but in the process she wore him down. This man with his gentle smile, his varied intellectual interests, and his lofty ideals, suffered in her society. She could not destroy his nobler nature, but his peace of mind and content she did contrive to ruin. And yet the beauty of his character, which she had ignored while he lived, exercised its influence over her after he was dead; and when she saw it reanimated in the sons, or looking, as if in reproachful reminiscence of the past, through the pure eyes of her daughter-in-law, she felt herself subdued and overawed.

I have said the stones thrown by the grandmother seemed to have struck home in the grandsons and to have lodged deep in their hearts. Look at the two men as they walk in the procession! The younger—the one in civilian dress—had a smile round his somewhat thin lips, a smile in his small eyes; but it seemed to me that it would hardly be safe to presume on this. He had owed his advancement to his father's political friends, and had learnt, early in life, to show himself subservient and grateful, even when there was little enough gratitude in his heart.

But now turn to the elder of the two young men. The same small head, the same low brow, but with more breadth in both. No smile *there* on mouth or eyes ; I could not conceive the wish to see him smile. Tall and lean like his brother, he had more bone and muscle ; and while both young men had an appearance of athletic power, as if they could have leaped over the hearse, the elder gave you the further impression that he was actually longing to perform some such feat. The younger brother's half languid gait, that told of bodily strength impaired by disuse, had become in the elder an impatient elasticity as if he moved on springs. His thoughts were clearly elsewhere ; his eyes wandered absently to and fro, and his pre-occupation was obvious enough to me later on, when I offered him my card and reminded him of our previous acquaintance.

Subsequently I got into conversation with several of the townsfolk, and I inquired what had become of the old lady. The question was received with a laugh, and the reply, volunteered eagerly by several voices at once, that she had survived till the previous year, and had died at the age of ninety-five. I could see that her character was pretty well understood. With no less eagerness these gossips also informed me that she had lived to see the house freed from the mortgage, one vineyard bought back, and the whole property cleared of encumbrance. All this was the result of the gratitude felt towards the martyred patriot whose praises were now on every tongue, since he had become the great glory of his native town; for his life and his brother's constituted practically its only sacrifice to the cause of Italian liberation.

And the old woman had lived long enough to see all this!

I inquired after the wives of the two heroes. I was told that the younger had succumbed to her troubles—in particular to the crowning stroke of misfortune which had deprived her of her only child, a daughter. But the elder, the mother of the two young Mansanas, was still living. When the townsfolk spoke of her, their faces became graver, their voices more solemn; the story was told by one of the bystanders with

occasional interpolations by the others, all however with a kind of seriousness which testified
to the influence this noble, high-souled woman
had obtained over them. I heard that she had
found means to communicate with her husband
while still in prison. She had been able to inform
him that the Garibaldians had arranged for a
rising in the town and an attack upon it from
without, and that they were waiting for Mansana
to escape in order that he might carry forward
the movement in Rome itself. Escape he did,
thanks to his own strength of will, and his wife's
acuteness and devotion. By her advice he
·feigned insanity; he screamed till his voice gave
way, and indeed, till his strength was exhausted,
for he had refused to touch food or drink. At
the imminent risk of death he persevered in this
pretence, till they sent him to an asylum for
lunatics. Here his wife was able to visit him,
and to arrange his flight. But when he had
escaped from captivity, he would not leave the
town; the important preparations on foot re-
quired his presence. His wife first nursed him
back to health and then took part in his
hazardous enterprise. What other man in his

place, after this long imprisonment, would have resisted the temptation to secure his freedom by crossing the frontier, which was scarcely more than two or three miles distant ? But one of those for whom he had risked life, and all that made life worth living, betrayed him. He was seized and imprisoned again ; and with his loss the greater part of the scheme, in which he had been concerned, came to nothing, or resulted only in defeat on the frontier, and in the condemnation of thousands of the patriots to captivity or the scaffold in the capital or the provincial towns. Before the hour of deliverance came, Mansana was beheaded and committed to his grave among the dead companions of his imprisonment, the thieves and murderers, who lay buried in the great Cemetery of the Malefactors, whence his bones had been removed this day.

And now his widow was there to await all that was left of him. Shrouded in her long dark mantle, she stood in front of the crowd that filled the flag-bedecked churchyard of Mansana's native town. The monumental tomb was finished, and that day, after the funeral ceremony was over, it was to be unveiled amid the thunder of cannon, answered by the blaze of bonfires from the mountains when darkness had set in.

Up towards the hill country, across the dusty yellow of the Campagna, our procession threaded its way. We passed from one mountain town to another ; and everywhere, far as the eye could travel, it lighted on bareheaded crowds of spectators. The populace from all the neighbouring villages had gathered on the line of route. Bands of music filled the narrow streets with sound, bunting and coloured cloths hung from the windows, wreaths were thrown as the procession passed, flowers were strewn before it, handkerchiefs waved, and not a few eyes gleamed bright through tears. So we came at last to Mansana's native place, where the enthusiasm with which we were received mounted to the highest pitch, and where our numbers were now augmented by large crowds of persons who had joined us on the march and accompanied us for a considerable distance.

The throng was densest in and about the churchyard. But as a foreigner I was courteously allowed to make my way through, and was enabled to take up my position not far from the widowed lady. Many of the bystanders were moved to tears to see her, standing there with that still gaze of hers upon the coffin, the funeral wreaths, the silent crowds. But she did not weep; for all this pomp and ceremony could not give her back what she had lost, nor could it add one jot to the honours her own heart had long since rendered to the dead. She looked upon it all as upon something she had seen and known years ago. How beautiful she still was, I thought; and that not merely because of the noble curves that time had not yet wholly swept from brow and cheek, nor because of the eyes, which once had been the loveliest in the town, and indeed were so even when I knew her thirteen years before, in spite of the many tears they had shed. But more than all this, was the halo of truth and purity that surrounded her form, her movements, her face, her expression. This was as visible to the beholder as light itself, and like the light it transfigured what it touched. Treachery and deceit felt its influence the moment they came beneath her glance, and before she had had occasion to utter a syllable.

Never shall I forget the meeting between her

and her sons. Both young men embraced and kissed her. She held each of them clasped in her arms for some moments as if she were praying over them. A deep hush fell on the spectators, and several men mechanically bared their heads. The younger Mansana, whom his mother had embraced first, drew back with his handkerchief at his eyes. The elder brother stood rooted to the spot when she had released him from her clasp. She looked long and intently upon him. Following her eyes, the gaze of the whole multitude was riveted upon him, while his cheek crimsoned under the ordeal. Her expression was full of an unfathomable insight, a sorrow beyond the reach of words. How often have I recalled it since ! But the son, even while he reddened, relaxed no whit the stern directness of his gaze at her, and it was clear enough that she felt obliged to avert her own eyes lest they should rouse him to defiant anger. Here, in sharp antithesis to one another, the two divergent tendencies and contrasted characteristics of their family stood revealed.

CHAPTER II

By the scene which I had witnessed my memory was long haunted ; but not so much by a recollection of the impressive part which the mother had played, as by the defiant countenance, the tall, muscular figure, and the athletic bearing, of the young officer of the Bersaglieri. I was curious to learn something of his history, and discovered, to my surprise, that it was the daring exploits of this son, which, by recalling attention to the father, were responsible for the tardy honours now accorded to the latter's memory. I felt I had struck upon something characteristically Italian. The father, the mother, the speeches, the procession, the beauties of the scene at the last ceremony in the graveyard, the watch-fires on the mountains—of all these not a word more was spoken. Until the moment that we separated in Rome itself, we were entertained with anecdotes concerning this officer of the Bersaglieri.

It seemed that as a boy he had served with Garibaldi, and had shown such promise that his father's friends had thought it worth while to send him to a military academy. As was the case with so many Italians in those days, he was entrusted with a command before he had passed his final examination; but as he speedily distinguished himself, he had not long to wait before obtaining his regular commission. One act of daring made his name known all over Italy, even before he had served in battle. He was out with a reconnoitring party, and chanced to be making his way, unaccompanied by any of his companions, to the summit of a wooded hill; when through the thicket, he saw a horse; then, catching sight of another, he drew nearer, and discovered a travelling carriage, and, finally, perceived a little group of persons—a lady and two servants—encamped in the long grass. He immediately recognised the lady; for, some days previously, she had driven up to the Italian advanced guard, and sought refuge from the enemy, of whom she professed great alarm. She had been allowed to pass through the lines; but instead of continuing her journey, she had evidently found her way back to this retreat by another route, and was now resting there with her attendants. The horses looked as if they had received severe treatment, and had been driven furiously all through the night; it was evident they could go no further without rest. All this Mansana took in at a glance.

It was a Sunday morning. The Italian troops were resting on the march; mass had just been celebrated, and the men were at breakfast, when the outposts suddenly saw young Mansana galloping towards them, carry a lady before him and with two riderless horses secured to his saddle-girth. The lady was a spy from the enemy's camp; her two attendants —officers of the enemy's force—were lying wounded in the forest. The lady was promptly recognised, and Mansana's "evviva" was echoed and re-echoed by a thousand voices. The camp was immediately broken up, as it was more than likely that the enemy was in dangerous proximity, and every one realised that the quick presence of mind of this Giuseppe Mansana alone had saved the whole vanguard from the trap prepared for them.

I have many more anecdotes to tell of him, but in order that they shall be properly appreciated, I must mention that he was universally considered the best fencer and gymnast in the army; on this point, I never, then or afterwards, heard more than one opinion.

Soon after the close of the war, while Mansana was quartered in Florence, a story was told, in one of the military *cafés*, of a certain Belgian officer, who, a couple of weeks previously, had been a frequent visitor to the place. It had been discovered that this officer was, in reality, in the Papal service, and that, on his return to Rome, he had amused himself and his comrades by giving insulting accounts of the Italian officers, whom, with few exceptions, he described as ignorant parade-puppets, chiefly distinguished for their childish vanity. This aroused great indignation amongst the officers of the garrison in Florence, and no sooner did young Mansana hear the tale than he straightway left the *café*, and applied to his colonel for leave of absence for six days. This being granted him, he went home, bought himself a suit of plain clothes, and started away, then and there, by

the shortest route for Rome. Crossing the
frontier where the woods were thickest, he found
himself three days afterwards in the Papal capital,
where, in the officers' *café* on the Piazza Colonna,
he quickly perceived his Belgian officer. He went
up to him, and quietly asked him to come outside. He then gave him his name, and re-
quested him to bring a friend, and follow to
some place beyond the city gates, in order that
the reputation of the Italian officers might be
vindicated by a duel. Mansana's reliance on
the honour of the Belgian left the latter no
alternative; without delay he found a friend,
and within three hours he was a dead man.

Young Mansana promptly set off on his
return journey, through the forests, to Florence.
He was careful not to mention where he had
spent his period of leave; but the news travelled
to Florence from Rome, and he was put under
arrest for having left the town, and for having,
besides, crossed the frontier without special permission. His brother officers celebrated his
release by giving a banquet in his honour, and
the king conferred on him a decoration.

Shortly after this he was stationed at Salerno.

It was the duty of the troops to help in the suppression of the smuggling which was being vigorously carried on along the coast; and Mansana, going out one day in civilian dress, to obtain information, discovered at a certain hostelry that a ship, with smuggled goods on board, was lying in the offing, out of sight of land, but with evident intention of making for the shore under cover of night. He went home, changed his clothes, took with him two trusty followers, and as evening came on, rowed out from the shore in a small, light boat. I heard this story told and confirmed on the spot; I have heard it since from other sources, and I have subsequently seen confirmatory accounts in the newspapers; but, notwithstanding all this corroboration, it is still inconceivable to me how Mansana, with only his two men, could have succeeded in boarding the smuggler and compelling her crew of sixteen to obey his orders, and bring their vessel to anchor in the roadstead.

After the taking of Rome, in which, and in the inundations which occurred soon afterwards, Mansana specially distinguished himself, he was sitting one evening outside the very *café* in which he had challenged the Belgian Papal officer. There he overheard some of his comrades, just returned from an entertainment, talking of a certain Hungarian. This gentleman had been drinking pretty freely, and, whilst under the influence of the insidious Italian wines, had boasted of the superiority of his compatriots ; and on being courteously contradicted he had worked himself up to the assertion that one Hungarian would be a match for three Italians. The officers, listening to this tale of brag, all laughed with the exception of Giuseppe Mansana, who at once inquired where the Hungarian could be found ? He asked the question in a tone of perfect unconcern, without even raising his eyes or taking his cigarette from his lips. He was told that the Hungarian had just been conducted home. Mansana rose to leave.

"Are you going ? " they asked.

"Yes, of course," he replied.

"But you are surely not going to the Hungarian ?" asked one of the officers good-humouredly.

But there was not much good-humour in Giuseppe Mansana.

" Where else should I be going ? " he replied curtly, as he left the *café*.

His friends followed him in the vain hope of persuading him that a drunken man could not reasonably be called to account for everything he might say. But Mansana's only answer was : " Have no fear, I know how to take all that into consideration."

The Hungarian lived, as the Italians say, *primo piano*—that is, on the second floor, in a large house in Fratina. The first-floor windows of Italian town houses, are, as a rule, protected by iron bars. Swinging himself up by these, Mansana, in less than a minute, was standing on the balcony outside the Hungarian's room. Smashing one of the panes of glass, he opened the window and disappeared within. The striking of a light was the next thing visible to his companions below. What happened next they were never able to discover ; they heard no further sound, and Mansana kept his own secret. All they knew was that after a few minutes, Mansana and the Hungarian—the latter in his shirt-sleeves—appeared upon the balcony ; and the Hungarian, in excellent French, acknowledged that he had taken more wine than was good for him that evening, and apologised for what he had said ; undoubtedly, an Italian was as good as a Hungarian any day. Mansana then descended the balcony in the same way as that by which he had gone up.

Anecdotes of every possible variety were showered upon us—anecdotes from the battlefield, the garrison, and society, including stories of athletic feats testifying to powers of endurance in running such as I have never heard equalled ; but I think that those I have already selected present a sufficiently vivid picture of a man in whom the combination of presence of mind, courage, and high sense of honour, with bodily strength, energy and general dexterity, was likely to excite among his friends high expectations as to his future, even whilst giving them some cause for grave anxiety.

How it came about that, during the following winter and spring, Giuseppe Mansana engaged the attention of thousands of persons, including that of the present writer, will appear in the course of our story.

CHAPTER III

As Giuseppe Mansana followed his father's bones to their last resting-place, looking, even on that sad and solemn occasion, as though he would fain leap over the funeral-car, it was plain enough that he was under the spell of his first burning dream of love. Later on, in the course of that same evening, he took the train to Ancona, where his regiment was quartered. There lived the woman he loved, and nothing but the sight of her could assuage the fire of passion that flamed in his heart.

Giuseppe Mansana was in love with a woman whose temperament was not dissimilar to his own: a woman who must be conquered, and who had captivated hundreds without herself yielding to the spell of any lover. Of her a local poet at Ancona, in a wild burst of passion, had written some verses to the following effect:

29

" The spirit of all evil things,
    The light that comes from Hell,
In your dark beauty, burns and stings,
    And holds me with its spell.

" In your deep eyes I see it shine,
    It dances in your veins like wine,
    Throbs in your smile, your glance of fire,
    Your siren laugh, that wakes desire.

" I know it ! yet 'tis better far,
    My empress, at your feet to lie,
Than be as other lovers are,
    And happy live, and peaceful die.

" Yea, better have loved thee and perished,
    Sphinx-woman, in darkness and tears,
Than be loved by another and cherished,
    Through the long, uneventful, dull years."

She was the daughter of an Austrian general
and of a lady who had belonged to one of the
noblest families in Ancona. That a woman in
this position should marry the chief of the hated
foreign garrison caused at the time a good deal
of resentment. And the indignation was, if
possible, increased by the fact that the husband
was quite an elderly man, while the bride was a
lovely girl of eighteen. Possibly she had been
tempted by the general's fortune, which was very
large, especially as she had lived in her ancestral

palace in a condition of absolute poverty. It is a state of affairs common enough in Italy, where the family palace is often held as mere trust-property by the occupant, who has no sufficient revenue provided out of the estate to keep it in proper order. This was the case in the present instance. Still there may have been some other attraction in the general besides his wealth ; for when he died, shortly after his daughter's birth, his widow went into complete retirement. She was never seen, except at church, and by the priests. The friends, who had broken with her at the time of her marriage, but who now showed themselves extremely willing to renew their acquaintance with the rich and beautiful young widow, she kept steadily at a distance.

Meanwhile Ancona became Italian, and the Austrian general's widow, ill at ease amid the festivities, the illuminations, and the patriotic celebrations of her native town, quitted it and settled in Rome, leaving her empty palace and her deserted villa and grounds to offer their silent protest. But once settled in Rome the Princess Leaney laid aside the black veil, which she had always worn since her husband's death, threw open her *salons*, where all the leaders of the Papal aristocracy were to be seen, and annually contributed large sums to the Peter's pence and other ecclesiastical funds. These actions—the first as well as the last—accentuated the feeling against her in Ancona, and thanks to the efforts of the agents of the "Liberal" party, the sentiment found its echo in Rome. Of this she was herself quite aware ; and indeed, when she drove out on Monte Pincio, in all her beauty and elegance, with her little daughter by her side, she could not fail to notice the hostile glances levelled at her by persons she recognised as inhabitants of her native town, as well as by others who were strangers to her. But this only roused in her a spirit of defiance ; she continued to show herself regularly on Monte Pincio, and she again returned to Ancona when the summer exodus from Rome set in. Once more she opened her palace as well as her villa, and passed most of her time in the latter residence in order to enjoy the sea-bathing. Though she was obliged to drive through the town to her house in the Corso, or to church, without exchanging greetings

with a single human being, she persisted in
taking this drive daily, When her daughter
grew older, she allowed her to be present at the
performances of plays and *tableaux vivants* at the
evening parties, which the priests promoted under
the patronage of the Bishop, in order to assist
the collection of Peter's pence in Ancona ; and
so great was the beauty of the daughter, and the
attractions of the mother, that many people would
go to these entertainments who otherwise would
certainly not have been seen there. As was
natural, the girl caught her mother's proud spirit
of defiance, and when, at the age of fourteen,
she was left motherless, this spirit developed
further, with such additions as youth and high
courage would be likely to suggest. Rumour
soon began to play with her name, more freely
and more critically than even it had done with
that of her mother, and her reputation extended
over a wider area ; for with an elderly lady as
chaperon—a stiff, decorous person, admirably
adapted for the office, who saw everything and
said nothing—she travelled a good deal in foreign
countries, from England to Egypt. But she so
arranged her movements that she always con-

trived to spend the summer in Ancona and the autumn in Rome.

In due course the latter town, like the former, had become Italian ; but in Rome, as well as in Ancona, she continued to display a kind of proud contempt for the governing faction, and particularly for those members of it who tried, by every possible artifice, to gain the heart of a lady at once so rich and so handsome. It was rumoured, indeed, that some of the younger noblemen had entered into a sort of agreement to either conquer her or crush her ; and whether there was any truth in the story or not, she certainly believed in it herself. The revenge she took upon those whom she suspected of designs upon her was to bring them to her feet by her fascinations, and then to repulse them scornfully ; to render them frantic, first with hope, afterwards with disappointment. When she appeared on the Corso and Monte Pincio, driving her own horses, it was in a sort of triumphal progress, with her captives bound, as it were, to her chariot wheels. If this was not obvious to the general public, she herself was fully conscious of it, and so, indeed, were her victims. She would have been killed, or have met with a fate worse than death itself, but for the protection of a group of staunch admirers, who formed a faithful and adoring body-guard round her. Among these worshippers was the poet whose verses have already been quoted. In Ancona, more particularly, the young officers of the garrison either sighed for her in secret, or regarded her with unconcealed dislike.

At the very time when Giuseppe Mansana's regiment had been ordered to Ancona, she had hit upon a new caprice. She absolutely declined to take part in the fashionable gathering which, every evening, was in the habit of assembling and promenading in the Corso. Here, under the light of the moon and stars and lamps, ladies were to be seen in evening toilettes, their faces half-hidden behind those fans they manipulated so dexterously ; gentlemen in uniform, or dressed in the last new summer fashion, strolled up and down, exchanging greetings and jests, gathering about the tables where their friends sat eating ices or drinking coffee, passing from one to the other, and finally settling down into their seats, when a quartette party began to sing, or some band of wandering musicians to play, with zither, flute, and guitar. In this function Theresa Leaney resolutely declined to take part. So far from aiding with her presence this daily display of the fashion, beauty, and elegance of the town, she had devised a plan to throw it into disorder and confusion.

At sunset, when the carriages of the fashionable world were turning homewards, she would drive out, with two unusually small Corsican ponies, which she had purchased that summer; and handling the reins herself, as she always did, she would pass through the streets of the town at a trot. She would choose the moment when the Corso was lighted up, and when the evening assembly was in full swing. On all sides friends and family groups were meeting; young men and maidens were exchanging stolen greetings; silent salutations were passing between wealthy patrons and their hangers-on; lovers, whose mistresses were absent, sighed their woes into the ears of confidants; officers tossed curt nods to their creditors, and high officials were receiving obsequious bows from their subordinates, anxiously hoping for the time when death would give them a chance of promotion. And then —before the young ladies had had time to exhibit their latest Paris gowns in the course of one turn up and one down the promenade, and just as admiring young clerks were opening the conversation with their charmers, while officers were collecting in groups to criticise faces and figures, and the more distinguished members of the local aristocracy were preparing to hold their customary little court —just then our arrogant young damsel, with her stiff, elderly companion sitting by her side, would dash into the very midst of the well-dressed crowd. The two ponies were kept at a smart trot ; and officers and young ladies, gentlemen and shop-assistants, family parties and whispering couples, had to separate in all haste, to avoid being driven over. A set of bells on the harness gave warning of the approach of the equipage before it was actually upon the saunterers, so that the police had no ground for interference. But this only intensified the irritation of those whom Theresa offended, first by declining to join their social circle, and secondly by breaking into it in this violent fashion.

On two evenings Giuseppe Mansana had gone

to the Corso, and both times he had almost been run over by this reckless charioteer. He was fairly astounded by her audacity, and promptly ascertained who she was. On the third evening, as Theresa Leaney halted her horses at the usual spot outside the city, where she was accustomed to breathe them before beginning the rapid drive through the streets and the Corso, a tall man in military uniform suddenly stood before her and saluted. " May I be permitted to introduce myself? My name is Giuseppe Mansana; I am an officer in the Bersaglieri, and I have made a bet that I will run a race with your two ponies from here to the town. I trust you do not object." It was nearly dusk, and under ordinary circumstances she could hardly have distinguished him clearly; but excitement will sometimes increase our powers of vision. Astonishment, and a certain amount of alarm—for there was something in the voice and bearing of this stranger that terrified her in spite of herself—gave her that courage which fear often inspires. Turning towards the small head and short face, which she could just discern through the twilight, she replied, "It appears to me that a gentleman would have asked my permission *before* he allowed himself to make such a wager ; but after all an Italian officer——" She broke off, for she herself was frightened at what she had intended to say, and there ensued an ominous silence, which rendered her still more uneasy. Then she heard a hollow voice—there was always something hollow in Mansana's deep tones—which said :

" I have laid the wager with myself, and, truth to tell, I intend to make the attempt whether you give me permission or not."

"What do you mean ? " said the girl, as she gathered up the reins. But the same moment she uttered a shriek, which was echoed more loudly by her chaperon, as both nearly fell from the carriage ; for with a long whip, that neither of them had noticed, the officer struck a cutting blow over the backs of the two ponies, which started forward with a bound. Two grooms, who sat behind their young mistress and had risen from their seats at a sign from her, to come to her assistance, were thrown back upon the ground. Neither of them could take part in the drive, which now began and was more exciting than long.

It has been said that Mansana's athletic accomplishments included great speed and endurance in running ; indeed, there was probably no other exercise in which his training had been so complete. He had no difficulty in keeping pace with the cobs, at any rate at the start, when the animals, firmly held in by their mistress, trotted slowly and uncertainly. Theresa, in her anger, was ready to risk anything rather than submit to such humiliation, and, besides, she was anxious to gain time till her servants could come up. But just as she was succeeding in stopping the horses, the whip came whizzing down across their backs, and again they plunged forward. No word or cry passed Theresa's lips, but she drew at the reins so hard and persistently that the horses came near to a halt, till the lash smote upon their flanks again. Twice was the effort to stop repeated, and twice frustrated in the same rude manner, till both the driver and the beaten ponies felt the futility of the attempt. All through this the elder woman had clung screaming to the girl, both arms thrown round her waist; now she sank forward, in a kind of swoon of terror, and had to be forcibly restrained from falling out of the carriage. A flood of anger and dismay swept over Theresa; for a time the horses, the road, were blurred before her eyes, and at last she could hardly tell whether she still held the reins or not. She had, in fact, allowed them to drop upon her lap; she took them up again, and with one arm thrown round the drooping figure of her chaperon, and both her hands grasping at the reins, she made yet another effort to regain command of the terrified ponies. But she soon perceived that they were now beyond all control. It had grown quite dark ; high in the air, above the undergrowth of bushes, the tall poplars by the roadside seemed to be moving swiftly onward, and keeping pace, as it were, with the carriage. She no longer knew where she was. The only object she could clearly distinguish, except the horses, was the tall figure at their side—the spectral form that towered above the little animals, and kept steadily abreast of them. Where were they going ? And like lightning the thought flashed upon her that they were not making for the town, that this stranger was not an officer, but a brigand, that she was being carried off to some distant hiding-place, and that presently the rest of the band would be upon her. In the agony of distress which this sudden apprehension raised, there broke from her the cry, " Stop, for God's sake. What is it you are doing ? Can you not see ——" she could say no more, for again she heard the lash whizzing through the air, and the crack of its stroke upon the backs of the horses, and felt herself whirled faster than ever along the road.

Swiftly as this wild flight itself, the thoughts chased one another through her mind.

" What does he mean to do ? Who is he ? Can he be one of those whom I have offended ?" A hasty succession of figures passed before her, but none of them at all resembled this man. But now the suggestion of revenge had seized hold upon her frightened imagination. What if this stranger had been deputed to take vengeance upon her for all her other victims ? And if this was revenge, then worse things yet were in store for her. The tinkle of the horses' bells cut through the rumbling of the wheels ; the sharp, shrill sound struck upon her like a cry of anguish, and in her terror she was ready to risk everything in a leap from the carriage. But no sooner did she relax her hold of her companion, than the latter rolled over in a senseless heap, and Theresa, in growing alarm and anxiety, could only lift up the fainting figure and support it across her lap. Thus she sat for a while, too perturbed for definite thought, till suddenly, at a turn of the road, she caught sight of the luminous haze that hung over the city, and for a moment felt that she was saved. But the sensation of relief passed like a flash, as the meaning of the whole scheme dawned upon her. This man was an emissary of vengeance from the Corso! And before the thought had assumed coherent shape in her mind, she cried out, " Ah ! no further ! no further ! "

The echo of her own beseeching words, the jangle of the horses' bells, the mad movement of the poplars alongside, were all she had for answer, as they dashed on. No word came from the silent shape in front. There coursed through her mind a forecast of her pitiful progress through the city, driven onward by the lash, her swooning companion dragging on her arms, the crowd lining the pavements to stare at her, the officers pressing forward to greet her with mocking applause and laughter; for that all this was planned by the officers, to wreak their anger upon her, she now felt certain. She bowed her head as if she were already in the midst of her tormentors. The next moment she could tell by the sound that the horses were slackening speed. They must be close to their destination ; but would they stop before they reached it ? She looked up with a sudden rush of awakened hope. She perceived why the pace had grown slower. Her captor had fallen back behind the horses ; he was now close beside her, and presently she found herself listening to his hurried, laboured breathing, until she could hear nothing else, and all her agonising fear fastened on it. What if this man should fall, with the blood streaming from his lips, in the Corso itself ? That blood would be upon her head, for it was her defiant pride which had challenged his desperate feat ; and his friends would tear her to pieces in their anger.

"Spare yourself," she implored, "I am con-quered—I yield."

But as if this attempt to soften him had roused him anew, he made a final effort. With two or three long strides he was abreast of the horses, who quickened their pace instinctively as they felt his approach, but not soon enough to escape a couple of swinging strokes from the whip.

And now clear before her shone the lights of the first gas-lamps, those round the Cavour memorial; presently they would be at the Corso and the miserable farce would begin. She felt a mastering desire to weep, and yet no tears came ; she could only bow her head upon her hands so that she might see nothing. Then of a sudden she heard his voice, though she could not distinguish the words; for the carriage was now rumbling over the paved causeway, and he was too exhausted to speak distinctly. She looked up, the man was gone ! Merciful heavens ! Had he fallen fainting to the earth ? Her blood froze in her veins at the thought, but her fears were needless. She saw him walk slowly away, through the Corso, past the Café Garibaldi. Then she herself passed into the Corso, her horses at the trot, the crowd parting to let her through. She bent still lower over the rigid form of her friend, as it lay across her lap ; shame and terror drove her onwards, as if with

45

a scourge.   A few minutes later, she was safely
within the courtyard of her palace.   Through
the open gateway the horses had swung at full
speed, so that it was a wonder the carriage was
not upset or dashed to pieces.   She was safe ;
but the strain had been too much for her, and
she fainted away.

An old servant stood awaiting her arrival.
He called for help, and the two ladies were
carried upstairs.   Presently the grooms who
had been thrown from the carriage came up and
related what had happened, so far at least as
they knew it themselves.   Ashamed and confused
by the reproaches which the old retainer showered
upon them for their clumsiness, they were only
too willing to follow his advice, which was to
hold their tongues, and say nothing about the
affair.   The horses had bolted, after a short halt,
just as the grooms were about to mount to their
seats.   That was the whole story.

CHAPTER IV

WHEN Princess Theresa Leaney came to herself again, all her strength and energy seemed gone from her. She would not rise, she scarcely touched her food, and allowed no one to remain near her. In silence her companion passed through the large mirror-room that adjoined the ante-room ; in silence she returned when her duties were accomplished, and when she entered the small Gothic apartment which the princess occupied near the centre of the palace, she was still careful to observe the same silence. The servants followed her example. This elderly chaperon of Theresa's had been brought up in a convent, and had come out into the world with an exaggerated estimate of her acquirements and position. But ten or fifteen years' experience of the selfishness and crude egoism of youth had tended to dissipate such sentiments, and she eventually took a situation as a sort of superior companion in an aristocratic family. Slights and humiliations were inevitable in her position, but she bore them in silence, learning, as she grew older, to put up with many things ; she grew reserved and taciturn, and applied herself diligently to the steady accumulation of money. With this object in view, she made a point of studying carefully the characters and habits of those she served, taking care that the information thus acquired should subsequently be of profit to both parties. It was her tactful knowledge of the character of the princess which had on this particular occasion enjoined that strict silence should be kept.

Suddenly, after the lapse of a few days, there came from the princess's little Gothic room the curt command, " Pack up," and subsequently this was followed by the intimation that a long journey was in prospect. A little later the princess herself appeared. Still silent and languid, she moved slowly about the rooms, arranged some trivial matters, wrote a letter or two, and disappeared again. Next day came forth the order, " This evening at seven o'clock," and punctually at six o'clock she herself emerged, dressed in black travelling costume, followed by her maid, also dressed for a journey. The companion stood in readiness, waiting, before giving the man-servant the final order to close the luggage, till the princess had bestowed an approving glance on the contents. She had not as yet ventured to speak to the princess since the carriage adventure, but now, approaching her casually, she remarked in a low voice, with her eyes fixed on the court-yard, "The town knows nothing beyond the fact that the horses bolted with us." This remark was greeted by a look of haughty displeasure, which gradually changed to one of surprise and finally dismay.

"Is he dead, then?" the princess asked, each word breathing her anxiety.

"No, I saw him an hour ago."

The companion had hitherto studiously avoided meeting the eye of the princess, and still kept gazing into the courtyard towards the stables, where the carriages and horses were being got ready for the journey. It was some time before she thought it advisable to look round, as the princess kept silent, and the servant made no movement; the latter, indeed, had studiously kept his eyes fixed upon the ground before him; but when, at last, she ventured a glance at her patroness, she saw in a moment that the information she had given had worked the desired effect.

Theresa's excited and overstrained imagination had, during those last few feverish days, shown her the whole town full of a scornful merriment at her expense; she had pictured the story, familiar even in Rome itself, and possibly, by means of the newspapers, known to the world at large; she had realised the humiliation and defeat which her inflexible and domineering pride had suffered in those few terrible moments. The thought was as painful to her as though she had been dragged literally through mire. And now, after all, no one but themselves and this Mansana knew of what had taken place. He had kept the secret. Truly a remarkable man !

The beautiful eyes of the princess flashed radiantly for a moment, then gradually melted into smiles, as with raised head and upright figure she paced awhile up and down the room, as far as the luggage and travelling impedimenta would allow ; then, lightly swinging her parasol, she said smilingly : "You can un-pack ; we shall not travel to-day," and hastily left the room.

An hour later, the companion received through the maid a message requesting her to get ready for a walk. She felt tempted to an expression of surprise, in answer to the look of astonishment with which the maid accompanied the command ; for during all the long and frequent visits they had paid to Ancona, the princess had never before consented to take part in the fashionable evening promenade ; but recollecting that in a servant such a look was an impertinence, she kept her feelings to herself. As Theresa entered the large pillared mirror-room, dressed for the promenade, she looked through the open door into the dimly-lighted ante-room, and saw her companion standing ready and awaiting her. The expression on the maid's face, as she followed to open and shut the door, was amply justified by the unusually handsome costume which the princess wore ; the companion, however, came up as though she were quite accustomed both to the expedition and to seeing the princess thus elaborately arrayed.

In a beautiful mauve silk gown, richly trimmed with lace, Theresa swept down the stairs. Her figure, instinct with vigour and strength, though perhaps a trifle too fully moulded yet gave an impression of supple grace, because of her height and the ease and lightness of her bearing. Contrary to the fashion, her hair was arranged in plaits, whilst behind her fluttered a long lace veil, which she wore fastened on one side by a brooch and by roses on the other. The large sleeves of her dress hung so loosely that even the long gloves scarcely covered her arms as she moved them when she used her fan. She stepped on briskly, not deigning to wait for her companion, whose business it was to be always at her side.

It was a lively evening on the promenade, the weather having cleared for the first time after several days of storm; and as the princess made her way through the crowd, the noisy hum of voices would momentarily cease, to burst out again, after she had passed, like a river dammed up and suddenly released.

Princess Theresa Leaney appearing at the evening promenade! Princess Theresa Leaney on the Corso! And in what guise! Radiant with a glow of beauty, wealth, and graciousness, she had greetings and a friendly word for every one; ladies she had known from childhood, tradesmen she had dealt with, officers and noblemen she had occasionally met—all received their share of favour. Though in this place, which in all Italy is the most renowned for the charms of its women, she might not have actually borne away the palm, she had, nevertheless, won for herself from far and near a reputation as one of the beauties of Ancona, and for many years the town had been prepared to fly her colours, and pay her homage, had she but desired it. And now, apparently, she did desire it! There was a look of ingratiating appeal in her eyes as she greeted "her people;" and in the bend of her head, as she acknowledged their salutes, there seemed a suggestion of conciliation.

One turn up and down the promenade sufficed to show her the change in the feeling of her "subjects" towards herself; and, seeing the members of one of the oldest aristocratic families of the place grouped in front of a *café* in the centre of the Corso, she ventured to stop and talk with them. She was politely greeted by the head of the family, an old gentleman, who was at first overwhelmed with surprise at her condescension ; but she quite understood how to put him at his ease, and the longer she sat and talked with him, the more enchanted he became, so that it was with a real pride and happiness that he introduced her to the rest of the fashionable world which gathered round them. She showed herself bright and witty and friendly to every one, distributing her favours impartially amongst the men and ladies, and it was not long before a tone of genuine gaiety prevailed. The group of which she was the centre increased to such an extent, that finally, when she rose to go home, she found herself followed, in a sort of triumphal procession, by quite a crowd of excited friends and admirers, all talking at the top of their voices. It might truly have been said that the Corso that evening was the scene of a general reconciliation between the aristocratic society of the town and its fair daughter, and, judging from appearances, both parties seemed the happier for the change.

It was getting late in the evening when, still followed by her retinue of friends, she once more, for the third time, made an attempt to turn her back upon the ices and champagne which had aided the general festivities. She was not allowed a moment's peace ; and so, moving away slowly, and still in the highest spirits, they were passing up the street, when three officers, walking smartly and covered with dust, as though just returned from some expedition, came towards them. Immediately the companion, in a casual manner, sidled up to the princess and whispered in her ear. Theresa looked up, and at once recognised one of the figures. It was Mansana ! Quietly, without attracting attention, the companion contrived to change places with the princess, who now was obliged to pass so close to the officers that the nearest of them must have grazed her dress with his sword, had he not chosen to step aside. This officer was Mansana.

They were beyond the shadows of the houses,

where the light fell full upon them, and she saw at once that he had recognised her; she observed, too, his astonishment, but she also noticed that the short, powerful face resolutely sealed itself against all expression, and that the small deep-set eyes seemed purposely veiled; his tact and discretion evidently forbade any sign of recognition. In gratitude for this, and for the silence he had hitherto maintained, she gave him one look from the depth of her glowing, dark eyes—and he was vanquished.

A fire was kindled within him, which burst in flames of colour on his cheeks; he could no longer collect his thoughts to listen to the conversation of his brother officers, and he left them. No one could have thought it strange that he should return home in good time, as he had already arranged to start early that night by the fast train, in order to be present the next day, when his father's bones were to be removed from the Malefactors' graveyard to a tomb of honour in his native town.

CHAPTER V

WE have seen how Mansana bore himself in the
funeral procession the next day, and we know
now why he walked behind his father's bier with
that elastic gait, that buoyant and springy step.
He had expected to find in the woman he had
insulted, an implacable adversary, and was prepared to meet her enmity with disdain. But a
single glance in the Corso from the eyes of
Theresa Leaney, as she stood there in all her
triumphant brilliancy and beauty, had set up a
new image in his soul. It was the image of
Theresa herself as the radiant goddess and
mistress of his being. Before her majestic
purity, how false and empty seemed all the
calumnies he had heard! How vulgar and
insolent his own audacious attack upon her!
Was *this* the woman he had had the effrontery
to persecute, to annoy?

He pondered over the mental conditions which

could make him capable of such a profanation. Step by step he traced their development, in his own harsh experiences of life, as he followed his father's body to the grave. He traced them back indeed to that father himself, since it was from him that he had inherited the bitter and perilous self-confidence which had sunk deep into his heart, and grown and flourished there. Under such influences he had indulged, to the full, the crude, wilful, egoism which had made him a law unto himself and his own desires and impulses the only standard by which he tested his actions, even as his father had done before him.

How often he had seen his mother weep! How often that noble and beautiful lady, as she sat alone with her boys, had let her tears fall in silent reproach of the man who had sacrificed wife, children, fortune, in a feverish pursuit of shadows. Yes, of shadows; for what was it that urged him on but the obstinate pride, the ambition, the vindictiveness, which in the beginning are often associated with patriotism and in the end are apt to become its masters? Giuseppe Mansana understood this as he thought over his own case and that of hundreds of others who passed in review before his mind.

The music clashed, the cannon thundered, the air was heavy with flowers and quivering with " Evvivas " in honour of his dead father's memory.

And yet, thought the son, what an empty, sterile life it had been after all. Plot and prison, prison and plot ; with mother, wife, children, left to want, family estates sold, and nothing gained but the unquiet heart's alternations from suffering to revenge, from revenge to suffering again ! And *that*, he mused, was my legacy from him : the suffering, the hatred, and with it all the vacant, unfulfilled life.

Close round him gathered the elder Mansana's old companions ; they clasped his hand, they congratulated him on the honours paid to his father; they heaped praises on himself as one worthy to inherit a tradition so glorious.

And still his thoughts ran on. Yes, my life has been as hollow as his. The fierce joy of vengeance while the war lasted ; when it ended a restless striving after adventure, a vain ambition, a proud sense of invincible success, took possession of my life—brutal, self-absorbed, hollow, all of it. And he vowed that henceforward his comrades should have something else to talk about besides the latest wild exploit of Giuseppe Mansana ; and that he would keep before his mind a nobler ambition than the haughty satisfaction he derived from the consciousness that, whatever his own achievements might be, he never spoke of them or of himself.

As they drew nearer his father's native town, the demonstrations became more animated, and larger crowds poured forth to gaze at Giuseppe Mansana, the dead hero's son, already well known by reputation. But to that son himself, as he passed through the familiar haunts of his boyish days, it seemed as if he could perceive the figure of his grandmother sitting by the roadside and throwing stones at the procession as it went by. He could almost fancy the old woman aiming, in her impotent wrath, at that baneful influence which had trampled down her life, and with it, all she had gathered round her to make that life happy.

And so, when his mother's anxious, sorrow-laden eyes rested on his, he felt her glance almost as an insult. *She* could know nothing of the thoughts that had been passing through his mind, nor realise how his own life had shaped itself before him as the gloomy sequel to his father's. But why should she gaze at him with those anxious, troubled eyes, at the very moment when he had resolved to cut himself adrift from all the temptations of ambition ? The mute appeal awoke no answering softness in his breast, and he met it with a look of cold and obstinate negation.

CHAPTER VI

Two days later he was standing on the high ground near the wall, that surrounds the old Cathedral precincts in Ancona ; his attention was riveted neither on the battered red marble lions which support the columns of the porch, nor yet upon the beauties of the bay which lay beneath him. His eyes wandered indiscriminately over the sailing vessels and the laden boats and barges, and over the busy, bustling life of the arsenal and the quays, but his thoughts were in the great church he had just quitted ; for there he had seen *her*. A solemn ceremonial had brought Theresa to the Cathedral. He had caught sight of her as she knelt in prayer; she, too, had noticed him, and, what was more, had shown herself evidently pleased to see him, and had greeted him with that look of indescribable meaning which had charmed him that other evening on the Corso. He could not continue

gazing at her without making himself obtrusive
or attracting attention ; and, feeling the incense-
laden gloom of the cathedral atmosphere in-
tolerable, he had come outside into the free,
fresh air, where his thoughts could wander in
undisturbed harmony with the beauty of his
surroundings. He heard the sound of the
people pouring out of church behind him, and
watched them, in their carriages or on foot, winding down the steep road at his feet. He would not
look round, but waited persistently till he should
see her also, immediately below him. Suddenly
he heard footsteps, double footsteps, close behind
him ; his heart beat fast, a mist grew before his
eyes ; he dared not, for all the world, have turned
round at that moment. The footsteps stopped ;
some one was standing quite near to him, front-
ing the old wall. He knew, as by an instinct,
who it was, and, unless he would show himself
discourteous, could now no longer refrain from
turning round. She, in the meanwhile, had
stood looking out over the bay, the ships, the
sea, quick, however, to notice when he turned
towards her. Her cheeks flushed, and their
colour deepened as she said, smiling, " Pardon

me for taking this opportunity, but I chanced to see you, and was anxious to offer you my thanks."

She stopped short ; he saw that she had something more to say, but the words would not come, and he waited during what seemed to him an eternity, before she continued :

" Silence is sometimes the highest form of magnanimity—I thank you."

She bowed, and he took this opportunity of stealing another glance at her. How charming was her courteous movement ! How bewitching her smile as she turned to leave him, followed by her companion ! What grace in the inimitable walk, and in the exquisite figure, robed in its crimson velvet gown, across which her long veil fluttered playfully.

She walked in the direction of her carriage, which had been waiting for her some distance down the winding road, and now came to meet her, turning as it neared the upper wall. But before it reached her she heard rapid foot-steps, almost quickening to a run, following her. She looked round and waited, well knowing whose steps they were. She was amused at

his impulsive eagerness, and smiled, partly perhaps with an idea of putting him at his ease.

"I did not grasp your meaning at once," he
said as he saluted her, the colour deepening on
his sunburnt cheeks. " I should like you to
know that it was not consideration for you which
kept me silent, but regard for my own self-
respect. I do not wish to be credited with an
honour which is not my due. I beg you to
forgive my gross rudeness."

His deep voice trembled; he bowed his head.
Mansana was no orator, but the genuine earnest-
ness of his words and manner, and the emotion
evident in the hand which quivered as he raised
it to his cap in farewell salutation, produced on
the princess all the effect of real eloquence. Thus
it came to pass that Princess Leaney, charmed
by Mansana's candour, conceived a strong inclination to reward him—an inclination strengthened by thoughts of a great discovery she had
just made concerning herself. And so it also
happened that Princess Theresa left her carriage
waiting, and walked past it, with Captain
Mansana on one side of her, and the companion,
as usual, on the other. Nor was this all, for the

princess—still with Mansana at her side—walked back once more; and together, for more than a full hour, they strolled to and fro, with the old wall just above them and the glorious scenery at their feet. At last, however, she was in her carriage; she had driven away, and, at the turn where the steep and winding road led into the level highway, she had once again looked up to bow and smile in answer to his prolonged farewell salute. Yet, though more than another hour had passed since then, Mansana was still walking up and down alone. The bold curves and outlines of the bay, the green slopes of the mountain sides, the limitless expanse of deep blue sea, the distant sails, the curling wreaths of smoke in the horizon. . . . Ah! the untold beauties of this bay of Ancona. ·

In their unforeseen meeting on that memorable evening, she discovered in him traits of character and qualities not dissimilar to her own. She showed him that her earlier history and his had many points in common, while she confessed, too, the foolish obstinacy and restless ambition of her nature. He heard all this from her own lips with a joy he scarcely could conceal. His being seemed dominated by a hovering image of ideal beauty, shadowed, it is true, by faults and failings similar to his own, but enriched by a halo of grace and beauty which had power to draw even him within its rays. Ah! the bay of Ancona. How beautiful it was, with its curving shores, its waves tinged to a deep blue-black by every passing breeze, and, over all, a mellow tint which melted seawards into a misty, luminous haze!

CHAPTER VII

AFTER this encounter, Mansana might very well have gone to visit the princess at her palace, but he still hesitated, perhaps with the secret hope that she might make one more advance towards him. The kind of self-brooding vanity, which he had so long cherished in secret, can be carried to absurd extremes, and is apt to be at once too retiring and too exacting. His shy reserve forbade him to call upon her, in spite of her express invitation, and yet he was audacious enough to cherish a hope that she would seek him at the place where he had already met her. Every day he went to the Cathedral at the hour of mass, in the vain hope of seeing her again. When at length he did accidentally meet her, as she was walking along the promenade by the bay, he perceived that she was perplexed or offended—he could not tell which—by his neglect. Too late he understood that in his sensitive vanity he had ignored the common rules of ordinary courtesy, and he hastened to the Palace Leaney, and sent in his card.

A veritable museum of historic memories is one of these old Italian palaces, with a foundation wall laid in the days of the old Roman Empire, an interior building dating perhaps from the Middle Ages or the Transition period, and an external court with façades and porticoes of Renaissance or sixteenth-century work. Not less reminiscent of many bygone ages are the ornamentation and decorative details ; and in the rooms, statuary plundered from the Greek islands or brought by the Crusaders from Constantinople itself, contrasts oddly with pictures, *bric-à-brac*, and furniture in all possible styles, from that of the Byzantine epoch to that of the present day. A grand old mansion of this kind, such as can be found at its best in certain of the Italian seaports, seems to summarise the larger history of human civilisation as well as the private annals of a great family. All this was well calculated to produce a deep impression on the mind of a visitor, especially when that visitor was a man of the people, gifted with a keen faculty of observation ; and it served to throw round the woman who reigned in the noble halls, that bore witness to the ancient glories of her race, a kind of distinction that gave even to her friendliness a little air of queenly condescension, and added a touch of stateliness to her courtesy. Small need for her to keep at a distance, by any artificial restraint, the man who approached her with a conscious sense of embarrassment, increased by the magnificence of her surroundings. The confidence based on the few previous *rencontres* disappeared. With the thought of his unexpiated discourtesy weighing heavy on his conscience, he entered her presence, subdued, in spite of himself, by the sumptuous staircases, the lofty apartments, the storied walls, the sense of contact with a long historic past. If he had brought her too near him in the rash licence of his imagination, now, with that same imagination fluttered and confused, he fancied her even further from him than perhaps she really was.

No wonder he derived little satisfaction from this first visit to his princess. At her invitation he came again, but the sense of failure that had settled over him on the former occasion still clouded his spirits, and the second visit was as constrained and awkward as the other. When next he came, it was with his wounded vanity in arms against this humiliating embarrassment. She noticed it, and *he* noticed that it secretly amused her. She smiled, and all his self-conscious pride drew back in alarm. Yet he felt himself powerless. Here, and in her presence, he could not give his feelings vent, he could barely find a word to say. He suffered in silence, took his departure, and came again, only to discover that she was playing with his anguish. If for a moment she had permitted herself to be mastered by him, all the more intense was the delight she now felt in this conquest of her conqueror. She treated him as she had learnt how to treat others, and bore herself towards him with a fascinating, unapproachable superiority.

Never did captive lion tear at his iron bars as Giuseppe Mansana chafed when he felt himself caught in this silken mesh of formal courtesy and playful ceremony. Yet he could not keep away from her. His strength was exhausted under the strain of frenzied nights and days spent in frantic struggles that led to no result.

Heavy indeed was the humiliation that had fallen upon him. He could not bear to hear her speak of another man; he did not venture to utter her name lest he should betray his misery and expose himself to ridicule. It was agony to him to watch her in conversation with any one else, though he could hardly endure to be in her company, lest she should inflict some slight upon him. Not once but a hundred times a murderous impulse swept over him. He could have killed his mistress, together with the rival whom, for the moment, she chose to honour with her preference, but was forced instead to turn on his heel and depart in silent fury. Where would it all end? The thought took shape within his mind that it must lead to madness or to death, or perhaps to both. Yet, though he felt this, he was powerless to make head against his infatuation; and for hours at a time he would lie prone and motionless in futile contemplation of the helplessness that had unnerved him. Why not perish in some deed of fierce vengeance worthy of his past? Thoughts like this chased one another through his soul, like thunder-clouds over a mountain's brow, while he lay there, fettered by the heavy doom imperious Nature had cast upon him.

In this frame of mind he received a formal invitation from the princess. One of the most celebrated musicians in Europe, returning from a journey in the South in search of health, was passing through Ancona that autumn ; he took the opportunity to pay his respects to the Princess Leaney, who had made his acquaintance in Vienna. In his honour she invited all the fashionable world of the city to her *salon*. It was the first entertainment she had given at the palace, and it was on a scale worthy of her wealth and rank. The general air of animation which prevailed infected even the invalid Maestro himself, and induced him to sit down to the piano. As he struck the opening notes his audience felt drawn to one another by a magnetic bond of sympathetic interest, as people do who know that they are to be associated in the enjoyment of a rare artistic treat.

Stirred by the common impulse, Theresa lifted eloquent eyes in search of a responsive glance. They wandered round the circle of her guests, and lighted upon Mansana, who, absorbed in his own thoughts, had unconsciously placed himself in front of the audience, and was standing close beside the piano. The Master was playing a piece called " Longing," a melody that seemed like the cry of a soul seeking consolation from out of the deepest abysses of sorrow. He played it with the feeling of a man who had himself known what it was to be very near the brink of despair. Never had Theresa seen a human countenance with an expression such as Mansana's then wore. Its ordinary stern composure was exaggerated to an almost repulsive harshness ; but she could see tear after tear swiftly welling over his cheeks. All the energy of his resolute will seemed concentrated in the effort to retain his self-command, and yet it appeared that in spite of his desperate efforts the tears would come. It was such a picture of inward struggle, linked with the keenest mental anguish, as she had never looked upon before. She gazed intently at him, till her own head was whirling in a maze of confused sensations, the most definite of which was the fear that Mansana was on the point of fainting. She rose hastily from her seat; but luckily a loud burst of

applause recalled her to her senses, and drew off
general attention from her. She had time to
regain her composure, and to resume her seat
for a few moments, till she felt collected enough
to look up unconcernedly and breathe freely
again.

Then she observed that, though the music
was still going on, Mansana had quietly made
his way to a door and passed out of the *salon* ;
probably the salvo of plaudits had roused him,
as well as herself, to consciousness, and enabled
him to perceive that he was no longer master
of his feelings. Her anxiety stung her more
sharply than before. Heedless of the looks of
amazement cast upon her, she pressed through
the listening throng and made for the nearest
door. She hurried on as if to stay some imminent stroke of calamity, filled with a vague sense
of self-reproach and responsibility. She came
upon him as he stood in the ante-chamber ; he
had put on his *kepi*, and was just about to throw
his cloak round his shoulders. They were alone,
for all the servants had taken the liberty to join the
audience in the music-room. With a quick step
she went towards him.

"Captain Mansana!"

At the sound of his name he turned. Theresa's eyes were kindling with excitement; he noticed the delicious *abandon* with which she threw back, with both hands, the masses of loose hair from her forehead—a gesture habitual with her in moments of sudden decision, and one that flashed unconsciously upon the beholder all the rare beauty of her figure.

"Yesterday," she continued, "the new pair of Hungarian horses, of which I spoke to you lately, arrived here. To-morrow I should like them to have a trial. I want you to be kind enough to come and drive them for me. You will come, will you not?"

His face paled under the deep bronze of his skin; she could hear how fast his breath came and went. But he neither looked at her nor spoke; only with a low bow he signified his assent to her invitation. Then he laid his hand upon the great hasp of antique hammered ironwork that fastened the door, and threw it back with a clang.

"At four o'clock," she added hastily. He bowed again without looking up; but as he passed through the open doorway, he drew himself erect, turned full towards her, hat in hand, and gave her one glance of farewell. He saw the gaze of troubled inquiry which the strange significance of his expression not unnaturally provoked. For his face bore witness to the sudden flash of inspiration that shot across the brooding darkness of his soul. *Now* he knew how it was all to end.

CHAPTER VIII

By four o'clock the next day, Mansana was being conducted through the ante-room, mirror-room, and concert-hall, to one of the Gothic apartments in the interior of the palace, where scattered about on the various tables lay photographs of the princess' last journey. He was informed that the princess would be ready immediately.

She made her appearance in a kind of Hungarian or Polish costume; for the November weather was chilly, and unusually so that day. She wore a tightly fitting velvet gown, with sable-edged tunic, reaching to the knee; and her hair was loosely coiled beneath a large hat, also trimmed with sable, to match the dress.

She gave him her white-gloved hand, half hidden by the lace and sable trimmings of the dress, with a firm, trustful confidence, to which her eyes, her face, and every curve of her fine

figure seemed, as it were, to bear approving
testimony. "It was to be!" At any rate, it
seemed to him that she was anxious to show a
greater confidence than she actually felt, and
this impression was confirmed when, immediately afterwards, she suggested gently that,
perhaps, after all, the drive had better be post-
poned; the horses might still be nervous and
fidgety from their railway journey.

Mansana, however, calmly put aside her fears
with a frigid pleasantry. She scrutinised his
face, always singularly hard to read, but beyond
the expression of strained suffering which it
bore, it revealed nothing; his manner was
respectful, but more peremptory than it had
been of late. The companion made her appearance just at the moment that the carriage and
horses were announced. He offered the princess his arm; she accepted it, and as they went
down the stairs, looked up in his face again, and
fancied that she saw a gleam of triumph in his
eyes. A little nervously she seized a moment
when the restive horses were being quieted,
before they stepped into the carriage, and said
again :

"It is certainly too soon after their journey to be driving them. Would it not be better to postpone the expedition?"

Her voice implored him, and, with her hand laid beseechingly on his arm, she looked trustfully into his eyes. Under her glance his face changed ominously, and a dark look came into his eyes.

"I might have expected that you would be afraid to drive with me a second time!"

She felt the taunt. With cheeks burning crimson, she sprang into the carriage; the companion followed her, pale as death, but stiff and unbending as a bar of iron, whilst Mansana, with one bound, leapt to the box-seat. There was no place for a groom, the carriage being only a light curricle.

From the moment the horses received the signal to start, the danger of the enterprise was apparent. Both animals immediately reared, straining in opposite directions at the reins, and it was certainly more than a minute before Mansana could steer them through the gateway.

"God's will be done!" muttered the companion, in deadly fear, her eyes fixed on the two horses, as they reared, backed, reared again, then, receiving a cut from the whip, kicked out, swerved violently from one side to the other, received another cut from Mansana, jibbed, and then finally, after one more sharp sting from the lash, started forward. The rough handling of the whip certainly did not seem to answer in this case.

As they emerged into the public street, the horses, to whom everything about them had a strange and foreign look, trembled and stamped uneasily; the novelty of their surroundings, the many and various sounds, all new to them; the different colourings of costumes, and, above all, the strong southern light, which gave to everything an unaccustomed glare—all these combined to terrify the poor animals. Mansana's skill and strength, however, kept them well in hand up to the time when they passed the Cavour monument; but from that moment, little by little his hold on them relaxed.

He turned round to see the expression on the princess' face. Now it was his turn to rejoice, and hers to suffer.

What could have inspired her with the unlucky idea of arranging this drive? She had regretted it almost as soon as she had proposed it, and ever since that moment, the day before, when she had caught the flash of triumph in his eyes, she had felt certain that he meant to use the expedition as an opportunity for punishing her; and she felt, too, that he was not likely to deal more mercifully with her than he had done before. Why, then, was she sitting there at all? As she watched his every movement and each action of the horses, she asked herself this question over and over again; not that she expected to find an answer, but because her thoughts insisted on revolving mechanically round this idea.

Still at a sort of springing trot—the most rapid trot possible—on they went; the pace was not permitted to slacken. Presently Mansana looked round again. His eyes gleamed with exultation. It was a mere preliminary to what was now to follow. Swinging the whip high above his head, with deliberate and well-judged aim, he suddenly brought it, whizzing down upon the backs of the two horses, who no sooner heard the whistling in the air above

them, than instinctively they gave a great plunge
forward, and broke into a gallop.   Not a sound
was heard from the two who sat behind.   Mansana repeated the performance, and this time
with maddening effect upon the horses.· The
road at this point began to slope down towards
a stiff, steep hill; and precisely at this very
point, Mansana, for the third time, raised the
whip, swung it in lasso fashion round his head,
and brought it down upon the backs of the animals.
Such an act, at such a moment, showed Theresa,
as by a flash of instinct, that Mansana's object
was—not punishment of her, but death with
her !

If there is a faculty within us capable of
bearing witness to the divine origin of our souls,
it is the power our minds possess of embracing, .
in the fraction of a second, great spaces of time
and series of events.   In the short interval
between the bending of the whip above her and
its descent upon the horses' backs, she had not
only made her great discovery, but by the
strange new light this shed on past events,
had lived over again the whole course of their
acquaintanceship.   In the revelation of the

moment she understood the nature of this man's proud and reticent love—a love which could welcome death with joy, provided it was shared with the woman he adored ! She had, moreover, within this same brief second of time, framed a resolution and also put it into immediate action, for, as Mansana's whip descended, a voice behind him called, " Mansana ! " Not in a tone of fear or anger, but, as it were, with a wild cry of joy. He looked back. She was standing up, heedless of the hurricane pace at which they sped, with beaming face and outstretched arms. Quicker than words can tell, he once more faced the horses, flung away the whip, and wound the reins thrice about his arms, and, making full use of all his strength, pressed his feet firmly against the footboard. He wished now to live—not die —with her !

Then came a tug of war, for Mansana had determined that this bridal march of Death should be transformed to one of joyous Life.

On they rushed, through blinding clouds of dust—on—towards the brow of the steep hill. Mansana could just manage to hold up the foaming horses' heads, so that their long manes fluttered

like black wings behind them, but that was all.
He clutched the right rein fiercely with both
hands, in an effort to direct their headlong course
towards the middle of the road, preferring to take
this course even at the risk of a collision ; which,
however, would inevitably have given a dramatic
termination to the lives of the whole party. In
this effort he was successful, but still he could do
nothing to check the furious pace. He looked up,
and in the far distance fancied that he saw
moving objects—more and still more—drawing
nearer and still nearer towards them. On they
came—the whole road seemed blocked with them.
The distance between them lessened rapidly, and
Mansana realised that what they were approaching was one of those interminable droves of
cattle, making their way, as usual in the autumn,
towards the sea. He jumped up from his seat
and threw the reins in front of him. A
sharp cry from behind rang through the air,
followed by a still more piercing shriek as Mansana took a mighty leap, alighting on the back
of the off horse, while he firmly grasped the
bridle of the other. The horse he rode gave a
wild leap into the air, and the other, thus

violently thrown off his balance fell, was then dragged along for a space upon the outer shaft, till this snapped under the heavy strain, when finally the yoke strap which joined the two together also broke. Mansana's grasp of the bridle of the other horse helped him to save himself, and helped also, together with the dead weight of the fallen animal, to bring the whole cortege to a standstill. But the prostrate brute, feeling the carriage close upon him, struggled to free himself ; his companion reared, the near shaft broke, a splinter pierced Mansana in the side ; but thrusting himself in front of, or rather underneath the rearing animal, Mansana gripped him fiercely by the quivering nostrils, and in a moment reduced him to a state of lamb-like and trembling submission. The struggle was over, and he was now able to go to the assist-ance of the other helpless creature, which had meanwhile been making frantic and dangerous efforts to get free.

And now—smothered with dust, bleeding from his wound, his clothes all torn, his head uncovered —Mansana at last could venture to look round. He saw Theresa standing in the carriage, beside the open door. Possibly she may have intended to throw herself out, and have fallen backwards in the violent jolting of the carriage, and then subsequently have recovered her balance ; something of the sort may have happened to her, she herself knew not what. But one thing she did quickly realise ; she saw that he was standing near her safe and sound, with both trembling horses meekly submitting to his firm hold. She sprang from the carriage towards him ; he opened his arms and folded her to his breast. Locked close together, in one long embrace, were the two tall figures of the lovers—heart to heart, lip upon lip. As he clasped her to him, their very eyes and lips, as well as their arms, seemed riveted. Her eyes drooped at last beneath his gaze. A whispered " Theresa " was the first spoken word to part their lips for a moment.

Never did woman with greater joy accept the position of a worshipped sovereign than did Theresa that of adoring subject, when Mansana at last released her ; never did fugitive seek pardon for having struggled for freedom with eyes so radiant with happiness. And surely never before did princess set herself with such eager, tender zeal to the office of handmaiden, as did Theresa when she discovered Mansana's wound, and perceived his dust-covered and lacerated condition. With her own delicate white hands, and her fine lace handkerchief, and the pins she wore, she set to work to mend and dress and bandage, and with her eyes she healed and cured the wounds of which her presence rendered him unconscious. The intervals between her little services were filled as lovers well know how, and with a joy alternately silent and voluble. In the end they so entirely forgot the existence of carriage, horses, and companion, that they set off walking as though there were nothing left in the world but that they should forthwith disappear together in glad possession of their new-found happiness. From this dream they were awakened by a cry of alarm from the companion, and by the near approach of the slow-moving herds of cattle.

CHAPTER IX

ALL that day, and for days to come, the lovers lived under the glamour of their intoxicating dream of joy. It swept the fashionable world of Ancona into its current ; for the engagement had to be celebrated by a series of entertainments and country excursions. There was a fascinating element of strangeness and romance in the whole episode. On the one side there was Mansana's reputation, on the other, Theresa's wealth, rank, and personal attractions. That this invincible beauty should be plighted to the victorious young soldier, and that under circumstances which popular rumour exaggerated to an incredible extent, seemed to add a fresh interest to the princess in her new-born happiness, and to cast round her a magical charm.

Seen together, the lovers offered a piquant contrast. Both were tall, both walked well, and carried themselves with ease and dignity; but her face was a long oval, his short; her eyes were large and lustrous, his small and deep-set. In Theresa's face, the fine, straight nose, the voluptuous mouth, the nobly modelled chin, the cheeks that curved so exquisitely, framed in their border of night-black hair, compelled universal admiration; but Mansana, with his low brows, his thin, tight-locked lips, obstinate square jaw, and close-cropped wiry hair, was hardly accepted as a handsome man.   Striking, too, was the contrast between her undisguised happiness and brilliant gaiety, and his laconic reserve.   Yet neither she nor his friends would have wished him different, even in those days; for this reserve was characteristic of him.   Matters on which he would have staked his life were turned by him into mere every-day commonplaces, when he permitted himself to talk of them.

But as a rule, he hardly talked at all; and so neither Theresa nor their fashionable acquaintances observed that at this time—in the very crisis of his happiness—a great change was coming over him.

There is a kind of boundless submission, a

jealous desire to serve and minister to a lover, which may convert its object into a slave or a sort of powerless chattel, since it leaves him without a moment's freedom or a fragment of independence. He has but to express a casual wish, and instantly a dozen new plans are broached to secure what he is supposed to desire, and he is overwhelmed by a perfect storm of affectionate discussion. Then, too, there is that species of confidential intimacy, which works its way into the very guarded and secret chambers of the soul, which divines hidden motives and brings into the light the most cherished private thoughts; and this is apt to be embarrassing enough to a man accustomed to live his own life locked in his own ideas.

Such was now the case with Mansana. In the course of a few days he began to be affected by a sense of satiety; an intense exhaustion fell upon him, in the reaction from the alternate transports of despair and happiness through which he had lately passed, and added to his nervous irritability. There were moments when he shrank, not only from general society but from Theresa herself. He suffered the keenest self-reproach for what seemed to him black ingratitude, and with his customary frankness he finally confessed the whole truth to the princess. He gave her to understand what he had endured before their engagement, and how nearly he had succumbed to his mental anguish, and he pointed out that this surfeit of social gaiety and amusement was the exact opposite of that which he needed. His endurance was strained to its limits ; he could bear no more.

Theresa was touched to the quick by his words. In a whirl of self-accusation she proposed the remedy: Rest for him, travel for herself. She would take a trip to Rome and to Hungary to make her arrangements for the wedding, whilst he might go to a small mountain fortress in the South, where he could exchange for a couple of months with an officer who would be glad of the chance of staying at Ancona. With her usual impetuous energy she managed to get all the preparations completed in hot haste, and in two days both of them had left the city. They parted with an emotion which on her side was affecting, and on his, too, was genuinely sincere, for her passionate devotion touched his feelings deeply.

And yet no sooner was he left to himself, first on the journey and then in his new garrison, than he relapsed into a state of apathy. Almost the sole impression of Theresa that remained on his brain was one of tumultuous agitation. He could not even muster courage to open the letters which came from her; the thought of their possible vehemence shook his nerves. Once a day she telegraphed or wrote to him, and the task of replying to all these missives weighed so heavily on his spirits that it drove him from his quarters, where so many unfulfilled obligations lay in wait for him. As soon as he was released from his military duties, he would hurry out into the woods and hills that overhung the little town, which was situated amidst scenery exceptionally wild and beautiful.

Pondering over his engagement in these country rambles, it began to look illusory and disappointing. True, his promised bride could call herself Princess, but in Italy that lofty title has not quite the charm that attaches to it in other countries. Princes and princesses are too common, and the position of a good many of them is a little doubtful. Nor was he greatly attracted by the wealth Theresa had inherited from her father, since her mother had gained her share in it by deserting the national cause during the period of Italy's abasement. No doubt there was Theresa's undoubted beauty; but that was evanescent, and the lady already showed signs of a too rapidly ripening maturity. Their romantic engagement could not blot out of his mind the memory of the long humiliation she had compelled him to endure, or the subsequent display of overstrained excitement in her which had provoked him to a revulsion of feeling. In calmer moments a pleasanter picture rose before his mind; but then again his pride would take alarm and whisper that in this unequal union he must always be the subordinate partner, or perhaps that he would again become the sport of her caprices, as he had been before.

After his long morning rambles among the hills he usually sat down to rest on a bench placed under an old olive-tree, a short distance above the town, and afterwards walked back to breakfast. One morning two persons—an elderly gentleman

and a young lady—took their places on the
bench as he rose to go. The same thing
happened the next morning at the same time.
On the following day he lingered, not un-
willingly, a little longer—long enough to observe
what the lady was like and to exchange a word
or two with her companion. Italians glide
easily into conversation and acquaintance, and
Mansana ascertained without difficulty that the
old gentleman was a pensioned official of the
preceding *régime*, and that the young lady was
his daughter—a girl of about fifteen, fresh from
a convent school. She sat close by her father's
side, and spoke scarcely more than a few words—
just enough to reveal the exquisite sweetness of
her voice.

Afterwards Mansana met the pair daily, and
the meetings were no longer accidental ; he
waited on the hill-side till he saw them ascending
from the town, and then made his way to the
bench. He enjoyed the quiet friendliness of
their manner. The old gentleman talked willingly
enough, though with a certain caution, about
politics. When Mansana had listened to his remarks, he would say a few words to the daughter.

The girl's growing likeness to her father was easy to trace. There was a sort of wrinkled fulness in the old face, which showed that its owner had once been a man of the sleek, rotund type. The daughter's small, plump figure promised to develop in that direction; but at present it had only a soft and budding roundness of contour, that looked charming in the simple morning-dress, in which alone Mansana had seen her. The father's eyes had lost their colour and fire; the daughter's were half-hidden by down-drooping eyelids, and a slight bend of the head. The little maiden's face and her whole personality had a curious attraction for him in their tranquil meetings. Her hair was arranged with scrupulous exactitude each day, in the very latest fashionable style—a token of the convent-bred child's artless delight at being allowed to share in the vanities of this carnal world. The little dimpled hands, that sat so daintily on the trim wrists, were always busy with some fancy work, which the bent head and the downcast eyes followed intently. The eyes looked up when Mansana spoke to her, but usually with a side-long glance that yet did not quite avoid meeting

his ; and through them peeped timidly the un-
developed childish soul, half shy, half glad, but
wholly curious to look upon this strange new
world and its strange creature, man. The more
one tries to peer into such veiled, down-drooping
eyes, the more do they fascinate, since they still
withhold a part of their mystery. What her eyes
held—and there was often a roguish gleam in
the corners—and in particular what thoughts of
himself they hid, Mansana would have given
much to know. And it was with the express
purpose of breaking through her reserve that he
spoke of himself with more freedom than was at
all customary with him. It delighted him to see
her cheeks dimpling as he talked, and the pretty
quiver, that never quite left the tiny mouth, red
and sweet as an unplucked berry. It pleased
him still more when she began to talk to him, in
a voice whose fresh, unsullied ring stirred his
senses like the trill of birds on a glowing summer
morning. Then she took to questioning him,
with bashful inquisitiveness, upon the details of
his approaching marriage. Her thoughts about
engagements and honeymooning, not openly
expressed, but evident enough from the tenor

of her eager inquiries, seemed to him so charming that the engagement began to regain its old attraction in his eyes. Thanks to her, some ten or twelve days after Mansana's departure, Theresa actually received a letter from him, which was followed by others. He was no master of the pen, and his letters were as laconic as his talk; but he wrote affectionately, and that again was due to his new friend. If he now sat down regularly after breakfast to write to Theresa it was because earlier in the morning he had enjoyed one of those frank conversations with the girl; and with the fresh grace of the young figure, the busy little hands intent on their work, and the sympathetic play of lips, eyes, and dimples, in his thoughts, and the tones of the exquisite voice still ringing in his ears, he began once more to taste the joy of life and to feel the old yearning stir in him again.

Striking indeed was the contrast between this little friend and his superb Theresa, with all her beauty and accomplishments, and he felt it when he sat down at his writing-table to converse with his *fiancée*. He could no longer smile at her impetuosity; and yet how generously she made excuses for his silence. "No, I have not taken it amiss," she wrote. "Naturally you found it hard to write. You wanted rest—rest even from me. You ought not to have been made to feel that my letters were a burden to you from their vehemence. Forgive me. In this alone you are to blame, as I alone am to blame for the sufferings you have endured. I shall never forgive myself, but strive, all my life, to make amends to you for them."

Not one woman in a thousand would have had such ideas, or have written so generously. He was forced to admit that; and yet there came upon him again that constant sense of overstrain. To bring back the impression of tranquillity and composure, he wrote to her of Amanda Brandini, as his new friend was named. He repeated some remarks the girl had made about betrothal and marriage. As he wrote them down he felt their charm, and felt too that he had transcribed them rather skilfully, so that he read over his letter to himself with a certain degree of satisfaction.

Those bright morning meetings, which lightened the whole day for Mansana, were never followed by an invitation to call upon his friends at their own house. He respected them for this dignified reserve; but the meetings themselves fanned the flame of his longing to see Theresa again, and so one day, to her intense astonishment, the princess received a telegram, announcing that he was growing weary of his exile from her presence, and that he would be with her in Ancona in three days' time.

On the day he sent this telegram he happened to be strolling through a small *plaza*, where there was a *café*. He entered and called for something to quench his thirst. The place was new to him; and as he sat waiting to be served, he let his eyes wander round the little square, till they lighted on the form of Amanda Brandini upon the verandah of a house immediately opposite. This, then, was where she lived.

But she was not alone. Leaning against the balustrade by her side, and so close to her that he could almost have touched her lips with his, stood a smart young lieutenant. Earlier in the day he had been presented to Mansana, who had been informed that he was quartered at a neighbouring garrison, and that he was generally known by the *sobriquet* of "Amorino." And now this young Amorin's eyes were fastened on hers ; their smiling lips moved, but what they said could not be heard, and it seemed to Mansana as if they were whispering confidentially : a whispered talk that ran on unceasingly. Mansana felt the blood stand still at his heart as a sharp pang pricked through him. He rose and left the *café* and then returned, remembering that he had not paid for his untasted draught. When he looked up again to the balcony he was astonished to see that the pair there were engaged in a kind of struggle. The "Amorino" was evidently and rudely urging his advances upon the girl, and she kept him back, crimsoned with blushes. Her figure quivered with the agitation of the contest, her face glowed with excitement. The young officer's insolent advances were evidently provoking a tumult of resistance. Who had permitted this marauder to enter the fold ? Where was Amanda's father ?

CHAPTER X

THE next morning Mansana took care to be earlier than usual at the trysting-place ; but his two friends had also arrived before their accustomed time, as though they, as well as he, found pleasure in these meetings, and were anxious to make the most of them, especially now when only two more such opportunities were possible.

Mansana forced himself to go through the inevitable political preliminaries with the old man ; then turning suddenly to Amanda, changed the conversation by asking brusquely, " With whom were you disputing on the balcony last evening ? "

By way of answer her cheeks flushed with a bright, charming colour, as, in a manner peculiar to herself, she stole a sidelong glance into Mansana's face from underneath her lowered lids. Seeing her blushes, and little knowing how easily and quickly a young girl's colour comes and goes, Mansana's own cheeks grew pale. This frightened her; and as he saw this, he once again misinterpreted the meaning of her fear.

The girl's father, who had in the meanwhile been looking on in open-mouthed surprise, broke the silence by exclaiming, " Ah ! of course ! now I understand it ! It was Luigi, my nephew, Luigi Borghi ! He is staying in the town for a couple of days, in order to be present at the city festival. Ha, ha ! he's a gay youth, is Luigi ! "

Mansana waited with impatience till he was alone again, then started hurriedly in quest of Major Sardi, the friend for whose companionship he had specially selected this garrison. He would discover from him details of Luigi's past career. These were not favourable. Mansana thereupon, without hesitation, made straight for the hotel where the young man was lodging.

Luigi had just risen ; he greeted Mansana with the deference due to a superior officer, and after both were seated, Mansana began abruptly : " I am leaving this town to-morrow to make ready for my marriage, which is shortly to take place. I mention this that you may not misunderstand my motive in speaking to you as I am about to do. I have, during my short sojourn in this town, conceived a strong friendship for a certain young and guileless girl, by name Amanda Brandini."

" Amanda ! Yes ! "

" Amanda is your cousin ? "

" She is."

" I wish to know, is this the only relation-ship in which you stand to her? In other words, tell me plainly, is it your intention to marry her ? "

" Well, no ! but———"

" I ask you this question as one gentleman of another; you are at liberty to withhold your answer at your discretion."

" I perfectly understand; but I have no hesi-tation in repeating that it is not my intention to make Amanda my wife. She—well—she is not rich enough for me."

" Very good ! Why then, may I ask, do you visit so frequently at her house ? And why do you deliberately deceive her as to your intentions and fill her mind with ideas and sentiments which are meaningless, to say the least of it, to you ? "

" Am I to understand your last remark as a deliberate accusation ? "

" Undoubtedly ; it is a matter of public knowledge that you are a reckless libertine ! "

" Signor ! " exclaimed Luigi, as he rose indignantly.

The tall captain also rose to his feet.

" It is I," said the latter calmly, " I, Giuseppe Mansana, who make this assertion. I am at your service."

But the youthful Luigi Borghi was at an age when the love of life is strong, and he had no fancy for being run through the body by one of the most formidable duellists in the army ; so he kept his eyes fixed upon the ground in silence.

" Either you must pledge me your word never to enter her house again, nor make any attempt to see her, or you must take the consequences. I intend that this matter shall be settled before I leave. Why do you hesitate ? "

" Because, as an officer, I object to being compelled to——"

"To make a virtuous resolution? You may think yourself fortunate that I make this possible for you." Mansana paused, then added: "But perhaps I have been hasty. I ought first to have given you the chance of complying with my request, and have assured you that in that case you might henceforth regard me as a true and loyal friend."

"I deem it an honour to count such a distinguished officer among my friends, and shall in future reckon with pride on the comradeship of Captain Mansana."

"Very good! you pledge me your word?"

"Yes, I promise this."

"I am grateful; your hand upon it."

"With all my heart."

"Farewell!"

"Farewell!"

Two hours later Mansana was making his way down to the boulevard of the little town. Standing outside one of the shop windows, engaged in what Mansana judged, from the laughter which he could hear, to be a highly amusing conversation, were Luigi and Amanda. The father was inside the shop, evidently settling the account.

Neither of them noticed Mansana till he was close upon them, when the sudden sight of his white, livid face so scared Amanda that she instantly sought refuge with her father. The lieutenant, however, more horrified than she was at the unexpected apparition, stood, as it were, for an instant paralysed, then, moving involuntarily a step beyond Mansana's reach, found courage to stammer out : " Signor, I assure you I spoke to her at her own invitation only, and we— indeed, it was not at you we were laughing ! "

The sound of a sharp scream followed at that moment as Amanda, from her position of safety, suddenly saw Mansana, without a sound or even a warning movement, make a sort of spring towards the slight figure of her cousin.

It seemed to her like the leap of a leopard on its prey. Another instant and Luigi might be a dead man.

But the attention of the passers-by and of those within the shop had been arrested by Amanda's cry, and was now riveted upon herself, as she stood holding tightly by her father's arm. They gazed from her to her companions in the vain hope of discovering the cause of her alarm, but beyond the fact that two officers were standing quietly talking together outside, nothing remarkable was to be seen.

What was the excitement about? Curiosity soon collected a little crowd of idlers, who came clustering round Amanda, plying her with questions as to the meaning of it all.

Never in her life before had she been the object of so many inquisitive looks and eager questionings, and she was thoroughly frightened, whilst her father, himself speechless from bewilderment, was powerless to answer for her. At that moment Mansana came up, and making his way through the bystanders, with an air of quiet authority, offered her his arm. Thankfully she allowed him to lead her away from the gaping crowd, and her father gladly followed them. Mansana waited till they were out of earshot, then, turning to his companions, remarked : " I feel it my duty to inform you that your kinsman, Lieutenant Borghi, is a profligate, and I intend to see that he receives the chastisement he merits."

It was startling to Amanda to be told not only that Luigi was a profligate—though her notions as to the meaning of the term were somewhat vague

—but also that he was to receive castigation for some offence of which she was ignorant.

For once she allowed her eyes to open to their full extent, as, with a vain hope of gathering information, she kept them firmly fixed upon Mansana's.

Her lips were parted as in surprise; an uncontrollable curiosity had broken through her fears. He saw this clearly, and, angry as he had lately been, he could not resist a smile at her simple innocence and at the curious charm and beauty of her expression. And so, restored suddenly to good humour, Mansana gave way to a feeling of amusement at the old man, who stood looking for all the world like a half-frightened schoolboy listening to ghost stories in the dusk.

Anxious to show that he was thoroughly alive to the realities of the situation, he expressed a gratitude which culminated in an invitation to Mansana to accompany them home; and this Mansana accepted. Amanda—still half afraid lest something dreadful was about to happen—tried to disarm him by the smiling confidence with which she clung to him.

He began to have a suspicion of her motive,

and was amused, but this feeling wore away as he listened to the rippling melody of her laughing voice, as he looked at the sweet, rosy, dimpled mouth, and the clear, mystic, playful eyes peeping from their half-closed lids.   He gave himself up to the charm of her whole personality, and to the joy of feeling that this innocent, fresh creature was living, breathing close to him, and in that one moment he felt as though she were dedicated to him as his own.

Their last meeting was to take place on the following morning, but as he was not leaving till the evening of that day he suggested that very probably he might contrive to meet her once more in the afternoon.   And then he left her as one bewitched.   Under the tranquillising influence which her presence brought, he went that very afternoon to seek Luigi, found him in his apartments, and apologised.   He acknowledged that it was not Luigi's fault that he should by chance have met his cousin in the street, nor that she should have spoken to him ; and as regarded his having laughed——

"But we were not laughing at you," declared the terrified Amorin.

"And even if you were, you would have been almost justified. I can see now how ludicrous I made myself in my excitement."

He held out his hand to Luigi, who grasped it eagerly, and, after a few incoherent words, Mansana took his leave in the same spirit of confident self-satisfaction in which he had come. The little lieutenant, who throughout this interview had felt as though he were in the presence of his executioner, was now seized with a bewildering sense of joy at his departure. He jumped about the room, and broke into a loud peal of laughter. Mansana, who was still upon the staircase, heard the laughter, and stopped to listen. Luigi shuddered at the thought of his own carelessness, and the next moment heard some one knocking at the door. He was too much alarmed to say "Come in," but Mansana walked in without waiting for this.

"Was it you I heard laughing?" he asked.

"Upon my honour, no," answered Amorin, with a gesture of denial.

Mansana glanced briefly round the room and departed.

But no sooner was he gone than Luigi's

sense of elation and relief once more returned.
He could not control it, and as he did not dare
to shout or jump, and felt he must share his joy
with somebody, he went off to the military *café*,
where his little story created a welcome diversion
amongst his brother officers. To the accompani-
ment of their wine, they rained their witticisms
over the unfortunate captain, who on the eve of
his marriage with a princess could create a
scandal by falling in love with the daughter of
a little pensioner. Of all this Major Sardi,
Mansana's friend, was a witness.

Mansana's last meeting on the hill took place
next morning. It began long before the usual
time, and only ended when they reached
Amanda's door. According to his promise, he
came again in the afternoon to bid farewell.

Amanda talked with him of his approaching
wedding in a tone which was half playful
and half sentimental, precisely as her feelings
prompted her ; for to a well-brought-up Italian
girl, marriage is the herald of all earthly
bliss, the entrance to that happy state in which
uncertainty, restraint, and trouble cease, and
unchecked freedom, new dresses, drives, and

evenings at the opera, begin. And so her pretty chatter in some way re-awakened his old feeling of yearning for Theresa; her charm and personal attraction helped him still further to a realisation of his own approaching happiness, and he found himself confessing to her how much she herself had done towards this. A young girl's tears flow readily at words of praise, and our little maiden wept as she listened to Mansana's flattering talk. She thought it necessary in return, to tell him what confidence she too had felt in him; and though in her own heart she knew she had always, in his presence, been conscious of a slight sense of fear, she would not mention this. Then, as though in confirmation of her words, which were not so truthful as she would have wished, she gave him one of her smiling glances. The sunshine of her smile caught the glistening tear-drops on her cheeks, and framed a rainbow of indescribable beauty in Mansana's mind. He took her little round hand within both his as his farewell. A blush rose to her cheeks as he murmured something—he did not himself know what—and then he left her. He saw her pretty figure, arms, and

head, just above him on the stairs, and a minute
later on the balcony, as he looked up. He heard
from the other side of the square, a melodious
"farewell," listened for it once again, then turned
away down the side street. So absorbed was
he, that he had not noticed the approach of
Sardi, who was making straight towards him ;
indeed, he was only awakened to the fact by a
lusty slap upon the shoulder.

"Is it really true," asked Sardi, with a laugh,
"that you are in love with the little girl up yonder?
Upon my word, it would almost seem so ! "

Mansana's face grew copper red, his eyes
flashed, his breath came quickly as he answered :

"What are you talking about ? What have
you been told—that—— ? " He stopped wondering what he could be about to hear ; surely
no one could have—Luigi could never have——
"What did you say ? " he repeated.

"Upon my soul, you seem bewitched ! "

"What did you say ? " repeated Mansana,
with deepened colour, his brows knit, and one
hand laid, not too gently, upon the major's
shoulder.

It was now Sardi's turn to be offended.

Mansana's vehemence had so taken him by surprise, he had no time to consider what he should say, but in his own defence, and with a desire of still further irritating the unjustly aroused temper of his friend, he told him what people were already saying about him, and how the officers at the *café* were amusing themselves at his expense.

Mansana's anger knew no bounds. He swore that if Sardi would not at once reveal who had first started these reports, he must himself be answerable, and for a moment it seemed as though a challenge would be inevitable between the two friends. But Sardi, almost immediately recovering his composure, represented to Mansana what an ugly sensation it would create, were he to fight a duel with him, or with any one else, over such a subject as his relationship with Amanda Brandini, the very day before leaving to celebrate his wedding with the Princess Leaney.

Surely the best answer he could give to such a calumny would be to start at once, and make the princess his bride without delay. Thereupon followed a fresh ebullition from Mansana.

He would look after his own affairs, and protect his own reputation ; Sardi must give the names of his detractors ! The major saw no reason for concealment, and gave the names, one by one, merely adding quietly, that if Mansana felt an inclination to kill off all this small fry, he was quite welcome to the task !

Mansana was eager to make straight for the *café,* where all these officers would now be assembled. Sardi, however, convinced him of the folly of such a course.

Then, Mansana declared, he would at any rate seek Luigi. But Sardi undertook himself to carry the challenge to the lieutenant. " Though, after all," he added, " what is he to be challenged for ? "

"For what he has said of me," shouted Mansana.

"But what has he said of you ? That you are in love with Amanda Brandini ? Is this not true ? "

Now, had Mansana started on his journey without meeting Major Sardi, it is tolerably certain that he would, in two or three days' time, have been married to the Princess Leaney ;

whereas the following conversation now took place.

" Have you the boldness to assert that I love Amanda ? "

" I refuse to answer that ; but if you do not love her, what the devil does it concern you if the young whelp says so, or whether he cares for her himself ; or even whether he attempts to seduce her ? "

" You are a boor and a scoundrel to use such language ! "

" And what are you, pray, who can openly abuse a young man for the crime of talking and jesting with his cousin ? "

" Jesting with her ! " repeated Mansana scornfully, with clenched fists and knitted brows ; whilst Sardi interjected :

" Who is to look after her when you are gone ? "

" I shall not go ! " shouted Mansana.

" You will not go ? Have you lost your senses ? "

" I shall not go," repeated Mansana, his hands and arms raised above his head as if in confirmation of an oath.

Sardi was taken aback.

" Then you really do love her ? " he whispered.

Mansana recoiled. A groan, as from the strength of his whole frame, alarmed Sardi, who feared an attack of apoplexy, but after a brief struggle with himself, Mansana's countenance cleared, and slowly, as though unconsciously and to himself, he murmured :

" Yes, I love her ! " Then, turning to Sardi, he added : " And I shall not go away ! "

And from that moment he was like a driven hurricane of wind.

He turned and hurried away, in a storm of passion.

" Where are you making for ? " asked Sardi; as he hastened after him.

" I am going to Borghi."

" But we had agreed that I was to see him."

" Very well, then, go ! "

" But where are you going ? "

" To find Borghi ! " Then he added passionately, " I love her, and whoever tries to take her from me shall die ! " And again he turned to go.

"But does she love you?" shouted Sardi, quite forgetting that they were in the public street.

And once more raising his strong, sinewy hands above his head, Mansana answered, in a hollow voice:

"She *shall* love me!"

Sardi grew alarmed.

"Giuseppe, you are mad! You have been over excited, and it is only this unnatural condition of your mind which causes you to feel and speak like this. You are not yourself, Giuseppe! Do not run away from me! Don't you see that you are attracting the attention of the people in the street?"

At that Mansana stopped.

"Do you know what it is that makes me furious, Cornelius? It is the thought that I ever paid attention to those people in the street! I must needs hold my tongue, suffer, and be trampled on! This is what makes me furious."

He drew a step nearer Sardi.

"And now," he said, "I mean to proclaim it aloud to all the world; I love her!"

He actually shouted the words as he walked

on with proud step. Sardi followed, and, taking him by the arm, guided him quietly into a less frequented street. But Mansana paid no heed, and with loud voice and vigorous gesticulations, gave his secretly wounded egotism vent.

"After all, what should I gain," he cried, "by becoming the husband of the Princess Leaney, the steward of her ladyship's estates, the slave of her ladyship's caprices? Now, for the first time, I can acknowledge to myself the truth; such a life would have been unworthy of Giuseppe Mansana."

Sardi came to the conclusion that if Mansana could so belie the usual taciturnity and reserve of his nature as to bawl and shout in this outrageous manner, almost any mad feat might be possible; so, with an ingenuity and perseverance that did him credit, he sought to induce him to take a little journey, just to give time for the confused condition of his mind and his affairs to settle themselves. But he might as well have expected a hurricane to heed his words.

CHAPTER XI

THAT same evening, Amanda's curiosity was
stirred by receiving a letter conveyed to her with
every appearance of precaution. She struck
a light, and found that it came from Luigi—
the first he had ever sent to her—and thus it
ran :

" MY AMANDA,—There is a madman in pursuit
of me, and he threatens my life. An hour ago
he got me to swear solemnly, and to put my
hand to the oath, that I would renounce all
pretensions to you, and never even speak to you
again. I was a poltroon to submit to it. I
know that well enough, and you cannot despise
me more than I despise myself. But there is
this to be said : until I consented to that
declaration I never knew that I loved you.
Perhaps, indeed, I had not done so. At any

rate, now I know that I do love you—love you beyond measure, beyond bounds ; and in all the wide world there is no wretch more miserable than I am at this moment. But I cannot bring myself to believe that all is over between us, or that this monstrous agreement can be binding.

"All rests with you, Amanda, if you do not despise me too deeply. If you love me, then the madman can do nothing to you, and some day matters will happily mend for us. At present I am like one in a prison cell. I cannot move to release myself. But this I know : if you will not help me to escape from the toils I shall die. Amanda, give me a word, a sign. It is too perilous to write ; indeed, I know not how I shall convey these lines to your hands. At any rate, do not you attempt to send a letter to me. He might be on our traces even now.

"But to-morrow is the day of the *fête*. Be there in the neighbourhood of the band, and stay till I find you. Then, no words, but speak to me only with your eyes. If *they* are friendly I shall know enough. Ah, Amanda, all will

come right if you are mine. My own, my
Amanda.

"Till death,

"Your unhappy cousin,

"LUIGI."

No sooner had Amanda read this letter than
she felt that she loved Luigi. Never before had
she so much as hinted to herself a thought of
this, but now she loved him with all her soul.
She had no doubt on that point.

As to what Mansana had said about him, that
might be based on a misunderstanding; and as
to the promise Luigi had given, that, she thought,
was obviously a matter of no importance.
Young girls do not take a pledge of this kind
au pied de la lettre, when it seems to them
unreasonable. Besides, Mansana had left the
place.

So the next day came—the day of the *fête*.
It was a fine warm autumn morning, and Amanda
was up and ready betimes. The bands of music
had marched through the streets at sunrise,
and the cannon had thundered a salute. The
churches, decorated outside as well as within,

were crowded for the early service, and our little
Amanda was there by her father's side, tricked
out in her best holiday finery. She offered up a
prayer for Luigi, and as she rose from her knees
she practised her lips in a smile, the friendly
smile and deeply confiding glance that should
bring hope and comfort to her distressed adorer.
After the procession and the mid-day meal, she
hastened to take up her position at the appointed
place. The band had already begun to play in
the market square, but Amanda hurried her
father's customarily sedate pace so much that
they were enabled to find room among the very
first arrivals, though with the natural result that
after they had been standing there an hour they
found themselves wedged in the thickest of the
throng. She looked at her father's perspiring
face, and thought mournfully how unattractive
her own would look in Luigi's eyes. They
must make their way out, cost what it might;
that is, provided it did *not* cost a flower, or a
knot of ribbon, or even a vigorous effort, which
last would only have added to the embarrassing
redness of her burning cheeks. So she made
but little progress, and still grew hotter and

hotter. She heard the roll of the big drums and the boom of the trombones through the roar of voices and laughter all round her. She saw the campanile of the town hall and the clapper that hung below the great bell, and these last objects were all she could discern above the billows of living humanity that surged about and over her. Her father's suffering visage warned her how flurried and unpresentable she must be growing, and the poor little thing began to cry.

But Luigi had also been one of the first to find his way to the neighbourhood of the bandstand, and as the square in front of the guildhall of the little town was by no means extensive, it came about in due course that these two, who were seeking one another through the eddying mass of spectators, at last stood face to face. He glanced at her, and saw the deep blush and smile that shone through her tears. The blush he took for one of joy, the tears he thought were those of sympathy with his trouble, and the smile he welcomed as an earnest of what was to come. To her father in his distress and anxiety Luigi seemed like a guardian angel, and he called to him hastily, "Help us to get out of this, Luigi;" and Luigi applied himself to the task with vigour. It was a matter of some difficulty, and once or twice both Amanda and her father were in actual danger, so that the young man felt that he was acting quite an heroic part. With arms and shoulders at work he protected them, and with his eyes fixed on Amanda's he hung on her long, timid gaze. But he spoke no word, so he had not violated his promise. The consciousness of all this gave him a proud satisfaction. His bearing might well be noble, and he knew from the approving reflection in Amanda's eyes that in fact it did seem so to her.

But happiness in this world is doomed to be transient. A quarter of an hour previously Giuseppe Mansana had marked Luigi in the crowd, and with the instinct of jealousy he had been watching him from a distance—an easy enough matter for one of his height. The other, in his restless search, had constantly pressed forward, and thus had no suspicion of the danger that threatened him from behind; and now he was so deeply absorbed in his work of rescue—or rather in seeing his own gallant image flashed back from Amanda's eyes—that he did not notice Mansana till the captain's vulturine visage was scowling close beside his own, and he could feel his hot breath on his cheek.

Amanda uttered one of her little screams, her father was struck dumb with a sudden alarm, and Luigi contrived to disappear into the crowd.

The next moment Amanda had laid her arm through Mansana's, and he felt a warm little gloved hand on his, and saw two delicious, half-closed eyes, full of witchery, apprehension, and appeal, looking up into his face. They had just made their way out of the thickest of the throng so that conversation was possible, and he heard a voice, fit to call the angels into heaven, say: "Papa and I were in great danger. It was fortunate we had some one to help us," and he felt the gentle pressure of her hand.

Mansana had seen those same eyes dwelling on Luigi's, and there pulsed through his brain a thought destined to come back to him often enough afterwards, though for the moment it passed away as soon as it was formed. "What a silly, senseless business," he thought, "is all this in which I am entangled."

But the little prattler at his side ran on: "Poor Luigi found us in the crowd. Papa asked him to help us, and he did it without a word. Why, we have never even thanked him." Then directly after: "It is charming that you have not gone yet. You must come home with us, so that we can have a comfortable chat. We had such a pleasant one the last time."

Her round, young bosom fluttered under its silken prison, a glimpse of her dainty wrist showed white above her glove, the points of her tiny feet stole out provokingly beneath her petticoat, the rosy little mouth quivered with its burden of prattle and smiles, and the two half shaded eyes met his with shy confidence. Mansana walked home with them.

He did not mention Luigi's name, though it was fixed like the barb of an arrow in his heart, and fastened the closer the more exquisite she seemed. The strife between love and anguish robbed him of speech. But Amanda's sweet lips only moved the faster, while she made him sit down and brought out fruit, which she peeled herself and offered to him. She seemed so glad that their morning meetings need not yet come to an end ; she even suggested an excursion a little farther up the mountains on which they might adventure the next day, when she would bring breakfast with her. But still he could only utter a few monosyllables. He could not cloud this innocent idyll with the shadow of his suffering; and yet he was so torn by the struggle within him that he felt he could bear it no longer, and hastily took his departure.

Scarcely had the echo of his footsteps on the staircase died away, scarcely had the last greeting been waved to him from the balcony, than his smiling, invincible little charmer hastily shut the verandah windows and threw herself, sobbing, on her father's knees. The old man was not in the least surprised. His mind ran on the same thought as hers Mansana's parting glance, and indeed his whole bearing and manner, had filled the room with such an electric atmosphere of storm that he would hardly have been astonished if an actual explosion had occurred in the overcharged air. And when the girl whispered through her tears, "Father, we must get away," he could only reply, "Yes, yes, my child, indeed we must."

Their departure must be secret, and therefore it was necessary that it should take place that very night.

CHAPTER XII

GIUSEPPE MANSANA had gone to Borghi's quarters without finding him, and had searched for him in vain at the *café* frequented by the officers of the garrison, and later in the day, among the crowds of holiday-makers. During these wanderings he encountered many officers of his acquaintance, some of them accompanied by civilian friends, and it struck him that they relapsed into silence when they saw him, and spoke to one another in whispers as he passed them. Yet he felt that, whatever might be thought of the enterprise on which he was now embarked, he was in honour bound to carry it through successfully.

Late in the evening, worn out in mind and body, but alert and watchful, he sat down in front of the *café* which faced the Brandinis' apartments. There was a light in Amanda's window. She was putting together the few necessaries she proposed to take with her, for;

in order to give their journey the appearance of a short, casual trip, she had decided to leave their weightier luggage to be sent after them. But to Mansana it appeared more than likely that this lighted casement was intended to be a signal to some one. And presently it seemed as if his suspicions were correct. Wearied with the strain and fatigue of the day, Amanda stepped out upon the verandah, for a breath of fresh air. Her movements were very perceptible as she stood with her figure thrown into relief against the light within, and Mansana could see that she bent down to peer into the darkened square below her. Was she then expecting somebody who would come into the square from the side street? It seemed so, and presently steps were heard approaching from that direction. The newcomer was a man who kept close under the shadow of the houses, as he made his way to the foot of Amanda's balcony. As he passed under a street lamp, the light just enabled Mansana to catch a hurried glimpse of an officer's kepi, and a young, clean-shaven face, and he also noticed that Amanda bent still lower over the trellis of the verandah. A young girl in love—especially

when her love is clouded by danger—is apt to
imagine that she sees her lover's figure everywhere. The officer slackened his pace as his
eyes fell upon her, and under the balcony itself
he halted and looked up. Amanda retired hastily
from the verandah, closing the windows behind
her as she entered the room, and the officer
passed on. Was this their mode of arranging a
rendezvous? With rapid strides Mansana crossed
the square, but the stranger had already reached
the street that led out of it, and when Mansana
turned the corner in pursuit, he was no longer
in sight. In which house had he taken refuge?
Mansana could hardly knock up the whole street
to inquire, and was perforce obliged to abandon
the pursuit.

It was, in fact, a mere accident. A young
officer who happened to be lodging in the neighbouring street, paused for a moment under a
balcony, on which he saw a young lady standing
alone. Yet it was this trivial accident which
virtually determined Mansana's destiny.

He went to bed, not to sleep, but to pass the
night tossing restlessly in wakeful anguish, and
registering an oath, again and again, that before

the next day had passed she should be his or he would cease to live. But the next morning she did not appear at the trysting-place on the hillside. An hour he waited, but there was no sign of his friends, and he made his way to the house in which they lived. Before the door of their apartment he found an old woman carrying a tray with their breakfast, and to the door itself was fixed a sheet of paper. As Mansana lifted the knocker, the old woman said to him, "There seems to be no one within. Will you read the paper which hangs there?" Mansana did so:

" Gone away ; will write. B."

That was all. Heedless of the old woman, who called after him to ask what the paper said, he flung it from him and strode hastily away.

*   *   *   *   *

When the Princess Leaney arrived at Ancona on the following day, and found no Mansana there to greet her at the railway station, she was seized by a sudden indefinable apprehension. Hurrying

to the telegraph-office she sent him an anxiously
worded despatch, which testified to her alarm.
She went home, and waited for the answer,
her fears gaining ground as the minutes went
by. At length a messenger arrived with the
money that had been paid for the reply to
the telegram, and the information that the
message could not be delivered, as Captain
Mansana had quitted the town.

At this her fears completely overwhelmed her.
The self-reproach, under which she had lived for
days, assumed mountainous proportions, and its
shadow seemed to blot out all other thoughts.
She must find him wherever he was, talk to him,
care for him, yes, and nurse him, if, as she
gravely feared, there was need for that. The
same evening, with one servant only in attend-
ance, she was on the platform of the railway
station.

At dawn of the next day she was pacing
backwards and forwards at the junction where
the train from the West was to be met. She
paid no attention to her few fellow-travellers, in
whom, however, her self-absorption added to
the interest and curiosity she aroused as she

swept by them in her restless walk to and fro, with her long white fur cloak thrown back over her shoulders, and her loose hair and floating veil tangled together below her fur cap. In her large, wide-opened eyes, and in the whole face, there was the tense expression of overwrought emotion and exhaustion. In her walk she several times passed a tall lady, very simply dressed, who was looking intently into the luggage van, round which a busy little group had collected. Once, just as Theresa passed the group, an officer came up and spoke a few words to the lady, and in answer to a question addressed to him by one of the railway officials, replied with the word " Mansana."

The princess started.

" Mansana ? " she cried. " What——"

" Princess Leaney ? " exclaimed the officer, in accents of astonishment, as he saluted her.

" Is it you, Major Sardi ? " she answered, and added hastily : " But Mansana ? What of him ? You mentioned his name."

" Yes. This is his mother."

The Major presented the younger lady to the elder. As the mother drew her veil aside, the

calm, noble face that was revealed filled Theresa
with an instant sense of confidence and strength.
She threw herself into the lady's arms as if she
had found there a haven of refuge from all her
storms of anxiety and distress, and burst into a
convulsive fit of weeping.

The Signora Mansana said nothing, but she
soothed the agitated girl with a few gentle and
caressing touches of her hand, and stood waiting
quietly till her passion had spent itself and she
had regained her self-possession.   Presently
Theresa was sufficiently composed to ask where
Mansana was.

" That," answered the elder lady calmly, " we
none of us know."

" But we hope to find out before long," added
the Major.

White as a sheet, Theresa sprang up, and
looked from one to another.

" Tell me," she cried ; " what is it that has
happened ? "

Thoughtful and composed, the older woman,
who had been through so much of storm and
stress, said quietly :

" We have the same journey before us, I

imagine. Let us get a carriage to ourselves, and then we can talk matters over, and consider what is best to be done."

The suggestion was gratefully accepted and acted upon.

CHAPTER XIII

THE Brandinis had sought refuge in the house of
Nina Borghi, the old man's sister, and the mother
of Luigi, and it so happened that the train by
which they fled was the same in which the hero
Luigi also took his flight. It was, however,
only early the next morning, at a station, just
as Luigi was leaving the train, that they discovered each other. The unexpected sight of
them so put Luigi off his balance, he would have
passed them without speaking, but that the old
man seized him by the arm and obliged him to
listen to his tale of perplexity.

In reply, Luigi merely answered shortly, " Go
to my mother," and hurried away. The first
thing he did, however, on arriving at his own
garrison, was to go straight to the telegraph-
office, and, in a message teeming with excitement,
forewarn his mother of the arrival of her brother.
So alarming was the tone of the telegram, that

on receiving it the poor lady, who lived by herself outside Castellamere, near Naples, was seriously concerned, and her anxiety was not lessened by hearing from her brother and his daughter of the danger that was threatening them as well as her own son.

Captain Mansana had surmised that the Brandini family must have journeyed southwards, as there were night trains only on the southern lines. He therefore followed on their track, but, after two days spent in a vain attempt at finding a starting-point for further investigations, he turned back and made for the town where Luigi Borghi was stationed. He would probably know where the two were in hiding, and he should be made to give the information, or take the consequences.

As Mansana himself was well known, he set to work with great circumspection, in order that he might take Luigi unawares. He had already spent two days in the town before he came across the young officer in a street, where he had been watching for him, in one of the quiet little *cafés* frequented by the townsfolk.

To Mansana's surprise, Luigi was not so

much alarmed on seeing him as might have
been expected, and he further added to Mansana's astonishment by telling him without
reserve where the Brandini family was then
staying. This candour aroused Mansana's suspicions, and he pointed out to Luigi the possible
consequences of deception ; but the little lieutenant swore with unmoved countenance that he
was speaking truth, and Mansana, therefore, preferring to leave any further reckoning with Luigi
for the future, started by rail that same day for
the south.

What was his purpose ? It was still unshaken.
Amanda was to be his! For this reason only
had he spared Luigi. Since Amanda's flight,
so artfully carried out, his mind had chafed
under the determination that such an act should
not be allowed to go unpunished. He did not
love her, he said to himself. He hated her, and
for this very reason he would have possession
of her—or else——!

With these thoughts, from which he could not
free himself, were mingled visions of his fellow
officers laughing and scoffing at him. He had
been led by the nose and worsted by a little maiden

fresh from a convent, and a little lieutenant who had only just left school ! But he could not himself understand how it had come about that this contest with two insignificant children was the termination of his proud career. The image of the Princess, which lately, during his estrangement from her, had but seldom come into his mind, and then only to be angrily repulsed, seemed now, as the sense of his weakness and humiliation grew, to take stronger hold of him. She was the goal, the destiny of his life ! Such was the height to which she was now raised in his estimation. And in these high thoughts of her he was influenced, not by her rank, but by the glow and brilliancy of her ideas, and, as it were, the glamour that surrounded her whole being, exalted as she was by the universal admiration that was tendered her. But, as the charms of the Princess took firmer hold upon his mind, those of Amanda waned ; he did not even feel quite certain that she was not a little round-shouldered ; at any rate, he was able calmly to speculate upon the point. Those who have contrived to make us ridiculous in our own and other people's eyes are not always gainers by their efforts. So it happened that Mansana, having come to the conclusion that Amanda's figure was clumsy, her face and conversation insignificant, her voice monotonous, her hair extravagantly dressed, and her wheedling manner foolish and silly, began to ask himself if, after all, he would not be making himself still more ludicrous by trying to force such a person to become the Signora Mansana. Even more ridiculous did it seem that he should be willing to sacrifice himself on her account. What, then, was he to do? Return to the Princess? The road to her lay blocked—blocked a hundred thousand times, by his own pride! Break with Amanda and speed further afield, perhaps to the Spanish civil war? This would be the life of an adventurer, mere folly; he might almost as well commit suicide quietly at home. Should he retrace his steps and let things be as they were before? The Princess lost to him, the envy and admiration of his comrades foregone, his confidence in himself destroyed? There was no means of retreat open to him, except and only through the much despised Amanda, the cause of all his trouble. As her patron and protector, he might

at least pose as a victorious hero, and even though
the price that he must pay for such a position
were a life of unhappiness—well, if it must be
so, it must ! His honour would at any rate
be saved, and no one would ever be able to
penetrate the true secret of his heart. It would
surely redound to his credit that he had rejected
a rich princess for the daughter of an impover-
ished pensioner—that he had won her in open
combat, in combat even against her own desire.
But he had no sooner come to this conclusion
than his mind grew disturbed at the thought of
all the falsehoods which must be involved in the
preservation of this show of honour to the world.
He jumped up from his seat in the *coupé*, but
there were others in the carriage with him, and
he seated himself again. The train was carrying
him nearer and nearer to his goal ; and what a
goal ! The certain ruin of his whole life, as a
mere sacrifice to honour, although, even at the
best, it was extremely doubtful whether the
object of the sacrifice would be attained. The
merciful power of sleep intervened amid these
gloomy thoughts ; he slept and dreamed of his
mother, who, with her true and loving eyes,

seemed to watch over him like an angel. His tears fell fast till, at the moment when the train drew up, just outside Naples, he was awakened by an old man in the *coupé*, who could not bear to hear his sobs. Mansana sprang out of the carriage. It was a glorious morning, and the relentless clearness of the sky, bounded by the faintly defined outlines of the mountain chains, seemed to Mansana ruthlessly to expose his misery; he shivered in the chilly morning air, and returned to the atmosphere of the smoky engine, just then preparing to steam out again, to the rattling and racket of the noisy train, and to his own stifling thoughts.

A few minutes later, and they were coasting close beside the sea; what would he not have given for the train to have slipped from its rails and glided quietly, gently, out into the depths of the blue water. What peace ! What blessed release in such a death !

As the train stopped on reaching Naples, he hid himself in the corner of his carriage, lest in the crowd of loiterers there might be some one who knew and might recognise him. The day seemed to grow more and more beautiful as they threaded their way through the little sea-coast towns. The sun shone as warmly as on a summer's morning, and the bright rays refracted through the soft sea mist tinged with exquisite colour the mountains, sea and landscape. He left the train and drove towards his destination; then, dismissing the carriage, began to climb the steep rock-hewn steps leading to the place which was to be his journey's end. In those moments—with the waters of the Bay beneath him, and beyond the beautiful view of the distant islands like shapeless sea monsters guarding the approach, with the mountains capped by Vesuvius, and the towns gleaming white under the shimmer of the lazy smoke wreaths—he felt the reality of life. But it was not his own life spent in a vain chase after glory, a struggle for something he could not have defined, now that he knew it was to end in nothing; no, it was the power of a life such as was designed for him by the God of the vaulted heaven above, with the brightness of His glory that transfigures and irradiates everything, even to the end and limit ordained for mortality.

He made his way up towards the highest

146

point, and before long saw the house, surrounded by a high spiked railing, standing just beyond the brow of the hill. His heart beat fast; he knew there could be no mistake, as the road and the house answered exactly to the description just given him by his driver. No, there he was, for good or evil. And, before he had clearly realised what his actual feelings were, he caught sight of her—Amanda—dressed in her light morning gown, with a smile upon her lips, at something she had apparently heard or said, as she stepped out on to the balcony. But almost immediately, she saw him, and, giving one of her familiar little screams, ran inside the house again.

Just as an exhausted sportsman, brought unexpectedly in view of his long-hunted quarry, feels his lost buoyancy and energy return, so now Mansana felt suddenly within him an uncontrollable strength, an indomitable purpose, and, before he really knew what he was doing, he had reached the iron gate within the railing and, without stopping to ring and ask admission, had clambered over to the other side. His pent-up feelings relieved by this exertion, all his old

military instincts revived, he looked round, saw
the key attached to the inside fastening, and
promptly took it into his own possession. She
was now a prisoner in his hands. The door of
the house was only half closed ; he opened it, and
saw before him a large, bright, corridor, with
inlaid mosaic stone floor, stained-glass windows
which reflected curious lights and shadows on
the statuettes, and on the vases, which were filled
with flowers, palms and a variety of waving
plants. His eye caught sight of a couple of
quaint, old-fashioned settees, and on one of these
he noticed a straw hat with blue ribbons——did it
belong to her ?——and on the other, he saw a
parasol of a certain peculiar watered silk, with
carved, costly handle, set with a large blue stone.
Where had he seen this parasol before ? A
painful presentiment seized him, and, without
giving himself time to clear his recollection, he
hastily rang the bell. What he would do, he
must do quickly. But no one came in answer,
and there he stood, waiting, trembling, unable to
control himself. He grew desperate, he felt in-
action no longer endurable, he must do something
or give himself up for lost ; he rang the bell

again, and even this slight effort seemed to put
fresh vigour into his will ; come what might, he
would now lose or win, there should be no
middle course. And at that moment a door
opened, and from the room behind, the light
streamed into the inner entrance hall—and
showed him some one moving towards him. He
could only distinguish, through the coloured glass,
that she was tall and dressed in blue ; he heard
her shut the door behind her, and then everything
in the corridor grew clouded and confused. Who
was this ? A genuine fear came over him at a
sudden alarming thought ; was the house full of
people, and was he, perhaps, the victim of some
plot ? Who could tell in what confusion of
perplexing circumstances he might find himself
involved, what importunate individuals he might
come across here ? These thoughts stirred a
strong spirit of indignation and resistance. Was
it a fool's journey he had undertaken ? Not this
time ! He summoned all his powers of will and
determination, and was in the act of feeling in
his pocket to make sure of a weapon, when the
large door opened and through the doorway he
saw—yes, without a doubt it was—Theresa

Leaney, who, in a blue dress and with pale face, now drew nearer to him.

He stood motionless, agitated and dismayed.

The door between them stood wide open, and for an instant they remained one on either side of the threshold. Outside as well as within the house, all was as silent as themselves : and in this silence she held her right hand towards him. A sudden thrill shook him. He stretched out his arms, and, with a wailing, plaintive sound, as of a stringed instrument struck unawares, rushed into her wide-open arms. Then, taking her by both hands, he led her to the sofa, took her on his knee, buried his face in her bosom, and, pressing her tightly to him, lifted her in his strong arms, and finally, placing her beside him once again, with his head upon her breast, let his tears flow unrestrained. Still without a word of explanation, he threw himself upon his knees before her and gazed up into the face, that now smiled down on him in wondering admiration. Then, indeed—and the experience was all essential to his future happiness—did Giuseppe Mansana feel himself humiliated, vanquished! Purified and humbled, his eyes filled with gratitude, he looked up once more and was greeted silently, not by Theresa, but by his own mother, who stood behind her!

He and Theresa rose and turned towards her, and involuntarily he took her hands between his own, kissed them, and, sinking upon his knees, pressed them to his forehead. How much had he not lived through since that day when he had cast that look of proud defiance across his father's grave!

Mansana never got beyond the corridor of that house. When his mother and Theresa left him, to take farewell of their hostess, he hurried out before them, secretly anxious to replace a certain key within a gate, unseen; anxious also to fling from him, to the bottom of the sea, a revolver, the very thought of which now filled him with shame and remorse. This act accomplished, he sank down by the roadside, overwhelmed by emotions in which fear, joy, thankfulness and self-distrust were all inextricably mingled; and in this position, with his face buried in his hands, he was discovered by the other two, who, followed by the servant with the luggage, soon overtook him, on their way to the railway station. They travelled together, and in a few words Mansana heard how this meeting had come about. After information which Sardi had given them, they had sought Luigi, in the belief that he would know what had become of the Brandinis, and that, sooner or later, Mansana would be certain to make his way to them. Luigi's valiant candour had, no doubt, been due to his knowledge that Mansana's mother and Theresa had already discovered the Brandinis, and were even then with them.

Mansana listened to all this, but remained speechless still. His mother, watching him, grew anxious, and pleading her own fatigue as an excuse, insisted on resting awhile in Naples. She selected for this purpose an hotel that was in a quiet and secluded part of the town, and there at last, after much resistance, she succeeded in inducing Mansana to go to bed. Once asleep it seemed as though he would never wake, and it was not until late the following day that he at last opened his eyes. He found himself alone and felt confused and nervous, but a few small things about the room soon brought Theresa and his mother to his recollection, and with his thoughts on them, he lay back quietly and slept like a contented child. This time, however, it was not long before he was awakened by a feeling of hunger, and this satisfied, he slept again, almost unintermittently, for several days and nights. When at last he awoke he was quite calm, but oppressed by a gloomy reserve and desire to shrink more and more within himself. This was exactly what his mother had expected.

CHAPTER XIV

THE sequel shall be told in a letter written by Theresa Leaney to Mansana's mother, and sent from the princess's Hungarian estate not long after the events set forth in the last chapter:

" DEAREST MOTHER,

"At last you shall have a connected account of all that has happened since we parted at Naples. Excuse me if at times I repeat what I have told you already.

"Well, then, you must know that after our wedding Giuseppe's gloomy reserve was replaced by a devoted and humble zeal to do me service which made me anxious ; it seemed so strange in him. His old confidence and self-reliance did not return till after our visit to the town in which he had last been quartered. He quite understood why you wanted us to go there first of all; and how worthy of our love he showed

himself! Among his comrades he had, as it
were, to run the gauntlet; he faced the trial at
once, and with a courage which I think may
well be called heroic. And I should also like
to tell you a little about a certain young bride
who helped him then. You must understand
that never in her life had she seemed more
brilliant, more joyous, than at this time, when
it was a question of supporting this noble lover
through his days of humiliation. Her gestures,
her words, her whole bearing seemed to challenge
the question : ' Who dare say anything against
him when I say nothing ? '

" I have, I am afraid, still so much coquetry
left as to be half inclined to give you particulars
of my costumes on each of these three days. (I
had got my maid to come to me from Ancona
with some dresses.) But I will have the modesty
to forbear.

" And so it came about that, after those three
days of struggle in the mountain town, this
same young bride found herself loved as not
many women have ever been loved before ; for
there is power in that deep temperament, which
you, dear friend, have given him out of your

own perfect soul. But I must not forget to
praise the man Sardi ; for a man he is indeed !
He had done a most excellent service in giving
it to be understood that Mansana had been ill—
as, in fact, he was—and that you and I had
nursed him back to health. It was fortunate
that Mansana, who had already gained fame
among his comrades, had now laid up a store of
affection in their hearts on which he could make
many demands before it is exhausted. They
were determined to think well of Giuseppe Mansana. My dear husband felt that himself, and
it made him very humble, for he was oppressed
by the thought that he had not deserved all this
affection.

"In Ancona all went easily enough. The
main obstacles had been overcome. And now
—now at last—he is all mine, and I have for
my own the noblest character in the world,
cleansed and purified, the most considerate
husband, the most devoted companion, the
manliest lover that any Italian girl ever won.
Pardon the vehemence of my expressions. I
know you do not like them, but they *will* out.

"In Bologna—you see I hasten on—as we

were walking about, we happened to pass the
town hall. There two marble tablets hang,
inscribed with the names of those who fell in
the fight for the liberation of the city. I felt
a thrill pass through Giuseppe's arm ; and to
this circumstance I owe a conversation which
laid, deeper than ever, the foundations of our
union.

"You know, dearest mother, how my eyes
were opened to the wrong I did Giuseppe by my
odious, egotistical caprices ; they almost cost him
his life and both of us our happiness. You know
how my soul is constantly vexed by that state
of public feeling which breeds in us resentment,
hatred, unreasonable fanaticism, and a disgraceful
intolerance. An unnatural, unhealthy state of
opinion like this does more harm to society than
the most disastrous war, for it is impossible to
estimate how much it destroys of spiritual power
and efficiency, how many hearts it leaves empty,
how many families it lays waste. Believe me,
mother, that any nation which has achieved an
unrighteous conquest, and annexed what belongs
to others, makes all its citizens participators
in its wrong-doing. Not only does it relax the

moral fibre of every individual and add to the mischiefs done by private chicanery, violence, and robbery, and the harsh tyranny of officialism, but it robs the heart of its due rights in the family and society.

"Some silly verses were once written about me by an enamoured fool; not a word of truth was there in them. But now, my beloved mother, I feel that, if I had never met Giuseppe, what was said in those verses would have come to be true enough some time, for heartless and vain as I then was, heartless and vain I should have remained to the end! And why? Because the unhappy condition of public affairs had sown poison in my whole nature.

"And my confessions were met by Giuseppe's. His defiant, egotistical will had so mastered him that the most casual interference with his desires might have cost him his life, the merest accident have changed its whole course. But that same defiant will—in what atmosphere had it been fostered?

"We gave one another the fullest confidence that evening in Bologna, and then for the first time all doubts vanished and the future seemed absolutely secure.

"Here, on this estate of mine that I love, he has set to work. Here all was chaos, so that he has something on which his energies can be brought .to bear. He intends to resign his commission—he does not care any longer to play the soldier in peace time. He needs to be busy on definite objects, that lie near at hand, and if I divine rightly, the objects dearest to him are those most carefully hidden from the world. So, at any rate, it stands for the present; what events may develop I know not. But this I do know : let Italy be in danger, and he will place himself in the front rank, whatever the circumstances may be.

"God's blessing on you ! Come here soon ; you must see him in this active life of his, you must see him with me. Has any woman ever had so devoted a husband, so gallant a lover? Ah, I know you do not give me leave to talk in this extravagant vein. But I cannot help it, and I must tell you again that these are the words I feel I *must* use.

" I love you, and again and again I long to

embrace you, to kiss you, you dear mother, to whom I owe my happiness.

"Dearest, so hardly tried and proven, from whose eyes there streams a hymn of praise, from whose lips the words of help and comfort pour their waters of refreshment, we want you to bow your grey head over our happiness, that it may be blessed. Yes, you must let us learn from you, so that the evil days do not come too soon upon us.

"Your son's wife, your own, your loving

"THERESA."

MOTHER S HANDS

MOTHER'S HANDS

PART I

A STIRRING clang of swords, echoing from the glass roof of the station ; the ring of steel sounding through the hissing of steam, noise of laughter and talk, mingled with the dense dull sound of truck wheels, of footsteps, of luggage loading.

Every time a fresh succession of officers thronged the glass doors, the clang of swords rang sharply ; many artillery officers pressed through, and some infantry among them. All were making for the door of the same railway carriage, where a tall lady in black, with large, half-melancholy, half-imperious eyes, was standing and bowing. She bent her head slowly, a measured inclination, never more. The officers evidently came from manœuvres or parade. The King was in the town, as was indicated by the presence of some of his harbingers, that is to say, Swedish uniforms. Was he here in person ? Was he expected ?   No, for in that case there would have been others present besides the officers. But was that lady who stood at the carriage-door the person to whom they had come to bid farewell ?   Was she the wife of a cavalry officer then ?   No, that lady could scarcely have become what she was in the midst of a small military circle with horsey surroundings.   Besides, there was only respect in the greeting paid to her. The crowd was round some one who was standing on the platform and who could with difficulty be seen.   At that moment a white veil was waved aloft by a lady's gloved hand.   Was all this parade in honour of a lady after all ?

The long prognosticated war with Russia has not yet broken out.   There is probably time enough for that.   Many of these officers wear decorations in advance.   The colonel's manly breast bears at least eight of them.   He has much to make up.   Some of them—for instance, the two stately Swedes with their bland courtier eyes—are looking rather pale; perhaps they have been wounded as well as decorated in advance ?

The throng presses close round the carriage-door. So it is really a lady who is the object of all this bloodless fray, this pushing and pressing, this restless motion to and fro, the endlessly shifting phantasmagoria of necks and epaulettes, of features and bearded faces, this unanimous laughter to order?

Perhaps it is a princess? Good heavens, no! In that case they would have kept at a respectful distance; but here they are pressing closer and closer, until the entrance doors of the station are again crowded with uniforms and clanging swords, this time exclusively of cavalry, and a little man, very old, beaming with friendliness, sheer friendliness, nothing but friendliness, appears followed by a staff of old and young officers. Discipline and Court obsequiousness (in a small army in time of peace courtiers alone are advanced to the higher grades) have made the expression of his countenance as irreproachably correct as that of an old dial-plate. Only there are moustaches on the dials which two concealed strings at the back seem to jerk now into a smile, now back to gravity again.

Some one called out, "Make room for the

general," and in an instant a wide opening was made between two saluting semicircles, suddenly parted from each other.

Then it became possible to see the centre, which was formed of a group of ladies, foremost amongst them a tall girl in a light travelling costume and a white straw hat with a long white veil floating loosely over it. Her hands were full of flowers; she kept receiving more and more, which she handed through the crowd of ladies to her mother at the carriage-door, who laid them aside. Now it could be seen by every one that the two were mother and daughter. They were about the same height, the daughter, if anything, taller than her mother; they had the same large grey eyes, but with very different expression, although both proclaimed the wide range of their inward dominion. The mother's told of a deep comprehension of the contradictions and sufferings of life, the daughter's of an ardent nature, of restless aspiration, of warring forces which as yet had not found expression; they sparkled with triumph, through which there gleamed now and then a lightning flash of impatience. She was tall, slender, supple; her

movements seemed to reflect the radiance from
her eyes. It was not with their own eyes that
others saw her, but through the light of her
own. The look of energy in her face was a
powerful auxiliary in the spell her eyes exercised
over mankind. The mother's face was oval—of
pure outline and broad design ; the daughter's
was longer, sharper, the forehead higher and
framed by abundant light brown hair. Her
eyebrows were straight, her nose was aquiline,
her chin decided, her lips firmly cut. The
beauty of a Valkyrie, but not so defiant. Her
magnetic attraction came from enthusiasm, from
impulsiveness ; the flame in her eyes was light,
not heat. On the whole, the impression she
made was that she was borne up by invisible
forces ; all who came under the spell of that
impression seemed to be lifted up as well. She
talked to those on each side of her and in
front of her, she exchanged greetings, she
accepted flowers, and laughed ; those who
followed all these movements and changes felt
dazzled and bewildered as though they had
been watching waves in the sunshine.

Here was coquetry, perhaps, but with scarcely

a particle of the quality which singles out first one and then another. Not the faintest hint of allurement in the voice. There was no sort of enervating tenderness in that uninterrupted outpouring of health, capacity and joyousness.

This was the reason of her success—be it said to the credit of those who surrounded her. No one came first, no one was especially distinguished. They all received their meed, each after his kind.

This unanimous admiration and homage had sprung into existence the previous autumn, when the cavalry colonel, who had married her mother's sister, brought her back from Paris. This persistent candidate for the favour of men and women, who neglected no one except his own wife, had since the previous autumn had no more pressing or more important duty than to introduce his beautiful niece into society. He performed this office on horseback at her side, at balls at her side, at theatres and concerts at her side; he allowed no one else to take his place. He gave riding-parties in her honour, and the whole body of cavalry succumbed; he gave a ball in her honour at which half the assembly fell victims ; he took her to the officers' great banquet, and all the guests were smitten. As an old courtier he knew every move of the game ; she never appeared under unfavourable circumstances or to no purpose—on this occasion, every person present had been specially invited.

As to that, they all responded as willingly as possible ; but otherwise they would simply not have known of it, or the duty of the service might not have allowed them to come, or many of them would have considered it obtrusive. Now they were there by order ; to an officer the feeling that he is obeying an order adds sensibly to his enjoyment. Just look at the little general's back, as he kisses her hand, brings her greetings from his Majesty and gives her the bouquet which he himself has gathered for her in the morning ! Look at his back, I say ; it seems made to be patted and currycombed like a horse's. As he straightens himself again, he looks as happy in the beams from her eyes as a stiff-legged dog who sniffs meat under a napkin.

I have said that those present had the feeling,

and to an officer it is an agreeable one, of paying homage to order. That his Majesty himself had approved of her was a higher consecration yet. In the winter, out on the ice, he had deigned to fasten on her skates. It is true that she was not alone in this great distinction, or in becoming a member of the Royal Skating Club. The same honour was accorded to a great number of young girls besides. But every cavalry and artillery officer present—and there were many of them standing by when he knelt to fasten on her skates—considered it a special distinction offered to *their* lady.

Supported by the infantry, they sped after her over the glittering ice, without pause or stop— the Swedes as well. It needed but little stretch of fancy to picture her leading a sortie, to see in imagination horses, artillery, powder waggons, gliding over the mirror-like surface to the sound of horns, tramping of hoofs, and neighing of horses.

But, if she had presented no other aspect than this, all her beauty, exceptional as it was, would not have accomplished what we have just seen.

No, there was more than that. She was not

a woman to be seized, caught, held fast—it was like trying to take burning fire in one's hand. " She was neither for men nor women," some said of her, and the thought spurred them on. She eluded those who were in her presence, to the absent she seemed a meteor ; if memory is itself luminous, its glow is heightened by reflection from others.

This impression was strengthened by certain sayings of hers, some of which went the rounds.

When the King fastened on her skates he said gallantly : " You have the most charming little foot." " Yes, from to-day onwards," she replied.

A jovial colonel of artillery had dissipated a fortune on his comrades, on women, and on himself. "I lay my heart at your feet," he said. " Why, what would you have left to give away ? " she laughed, and gave him her hand for the polonaise.

She stopped in the polonaise before a young lieutenant, who turned scarlet. " You are one of those one could die for," he whispered.

She took his arm in a friendly manner. " Well, to live for me would probably be a bore for both of us."

She once went to the poet-in-ordinary of the regiment, a smart captain, to offer him a philippine. " Do you wish it ? " she asked. " There is one thing we all wish in respect to you," he answered, " but we can never manage to say it—what can the reason be ? " " To say what ? " she asked. " ' I love you.' " " Oh ! of course, they know that I should laugh at it," she laughed ; and offered him the half almond, and from that time they remained as good friends as ever.

But there were other kinds of sayings of hers which aroused yet more respect. A discussion was going on one day at the fireside about a certain gate which was called the " gate of truth " ; all who went through it were *obliged* to say what they thought, upon which she exclaimed : " Ah, then I should get to know what I think myself ! " One of those present said that those were exactly the words which the Danish Bishop Monrad had used when he heard of the gate. " And he was called a sphinx," added the speaker.

She sat quietly for a little while, became paler and paler, and then got up. Some time after she was found in an adjoining room weeping.

A learned man said at the dinner-table : "Those who are destined for something great know it from childhood." " Yes, but they know not for what !" she rejoined quickly. But then she became embarrassed. She tried to make a better thing of it, and said : " Some know it, and others don't," and then she became more abashed, and her embarrassment gave her an irresistible charm. People like to be conscious of the presence of lofty yearnings, even though they don't betray themselves.

In a confidential circle one evening people were talking of a young widow. " She is rejuvenating herself in a new love," said one.

" No, she is rather taking up a mission, a self-sacrificing mission," said another, who maintained that he knew her better.

" Well, I don't care which it is, provided she is devoting herself to something," said the first. " It is in devotion to something outside oneself that salvation is found—call it rejuvenation or what you will."

She had been listening to this. At first she

was indifferent, then she pricked up her ears, and finally her attention became riveted. Then she broke out: "No, the point is *not* to devote oneself." No one replied; it made a strange impression. Had anything happened, or was it a presentiment? Or was she thinking of something special, which no one present knew anything about? Or of something great for the sake of which it was worth waiting?

That which seems a little mysterious impresses people's minds. The better principled, the higher natured among the officers conceived respect for her. The feeling spread, and bore fruit. With disciplined wills, nothing takes root more quickly than respect.

There were certainly some who saw in her " devil take me!" the finest thoroughbred in Norway. Again there were those who would " by all the powers!" have given their hope of salvation for—I dare not say for what. But there were also those who thought of the times of chivalry and saw in their mind's eye the token the lady fastened on her true knight's breast as a consecration. A glance, a word from her, a dance with her, was the token.

Her glory fell upon them, there was something
nobler and more beautiful in them from that
moment.

How many there were who tried to draw her
from memory ! for she would not be photo-
graphed. It became a common pastime to draw
her profile ; some attained the greatest pro-
ficiency in the art. With a broomhandle in the
snow, with a match in cigar ashes, with skates
on the ice.

On the whole, it certainly was to the credit of
the regiment that she should be so universally and
unprecedentedly admired. Her uncle naturally
believed that he was the cause of it, but the
truth was that the way he advertised her would
have spoiled the whole thing for any one else.
She could endure the advertisement. And now
he had been put aside, without himself understanding how it had happened. He, who on
this day had organised the whole assembly, was
standing quivering with eagerness to be abreast
of the situation ; but he could not. It all went
on over his head, as though on the second storey.
He spurred himself up with exaggerated gaiety,
with abnormal energy, but he fell back, became

superfluous, became actually in the way. His wife laughed openly at him; he, who when he was abroad had hidden his wedding-ring in his pocket, and was ready to do the same thing again, was left lying in a pocket himself, like an empty cigar-case.

His wife was enchanted. From the beginning she had been alarmed when his miracle of a niece was brought into the house. The ostentatious partiality with which he introduced her into society produced results which went beyond his previsions. The crowd of worshippers kept growing greater and denser; after the episode with the King the enthusiasm rose to a kind of frenzy for a time. The rate of speed grew with the number; the colonel struggled to keep up like a broken-winded horse.

The bell rings a second time, there is a movement in the crowd, renewed clanking of spurs and swords, waving of hands, vociferous greetings. The heroine of the hour saluted, waved farewell for the thousandth time, gay words were spoken, smiles and bows were rapidly dispensed with cheerful grace. She was quite equal to the situation! The large,

checked travelling dress, the light hat with
the veil now hanging down from it, now floating in the wind, the haughty poise of the
head, the perfect figure, all this stood in the
sunshine of the homage round her. Surely it
was into a golden carriage drawn by white
doves that she was stepping? For the moment,
it was no farther than to her mother's side at
the open carriage-door, whence she smiled down
to the colonel on one side, the general on the
other, the ladies round them. Farther back still
her eyes fell on all the uplifted moustaches, the
light ones, the brown, the black, the dyed, the
thin moustaches, the thick, the curved, and the
inane, the drooping, the smartly curled. Among
that melancholy and shaggy crowd a few clean-
shaven faces looked like those of Swedish tenors.

"I hope you will have a pleasant journey,"
said the old general. The gallant horseman
was too discreet to try to say anything more
marked. "Thank you for the pleasure you
have given us this winter, my girl!" It was
the colonel's shrill voice. The bystanders
should see what a fatherly comrade he could be.
"Yes, I've often pitied you this winter, uncle,"

was the answer he received. "Now you must have a thorough rest in the summer!"

The colonel's wife laughed. It was the signal that all the rest must laugh.

The faces turned up towards her—most of them honest, good-natured, cheerful—almost every one of them reminded her of some amusing moment; an autumn and winter of riding-parties, skating, snow-shoeing, drives, balls, dinners, concerts; a wild dance over shining ice and drifting snow, or through a sea of light and music mingled with the ring of glasses, with laughter and animated talk. Not one of her recollections had anything un-pleasant about it. All stood out clear, brilliant as a parade of cavalry. A few proposals, amongst others some initiated by her worthy uncle, had vanished like a crowd of motes. She felt a grateful happiness for what she had experienced, for every one's goodness, till the very last moment. It overwhelmed her, it sparkled in her eyes, it shone in her eager manner, it was communicated to all those who stood beneath, and to the very flowers she held. But a feeling of having received too

much, far too much, was there the whole time.
Through it all a dread of future emptiness that
gave her an unendurable pang. If only it were
over !

The tickets were looked at, the doors shut,
she came forward again to the open window.
She held the flowers in one hand, her handkerchief in the other ; she was crying. The
youthful figure stood in the window as though
in a frame, her head, with the light hat and
veil, leaning out of it. Why in all the world
was such a picture not painted ?

Discipline forbade that any one should press
forward so long as the general, the colonel,
and the ladies formed a circle ; each one
remained in his place. Since those near the
window didn't speak, all were silent. They
saw her weeping, saw her bosom heave. *She*
saw them as in a mist, and it all became painful
to her. Could the whole thing be real ?

All of a sudden her tears were dried. A
compassionate soul beneath, who also felt the
painfulness of the situation, asked whether they
would reach home to-day, to which she eagerly
answered, "Yes." Then she remembered her

mother and made room for her at her side, but her mother would not come forward. There was even something in the mother's eyes which as she met them chilled and frightened her. She forgot it, for the whistle took the train away from the crowd, the whole circle fell back a step or two. Greetings were exchanged with increased cordiality, her handkerchief waved, the warmth in her eyes came back. They flashed again. All that could be seen of her called greetings to them, and they to her, as they followed. Now the lieutenants and all the young men were the foremost! Now feelings of a different sort found a different expression. The clashing of swords and spurs, the colours of the uniforms, the waving of arms, the tramping of feet made her dizzy. With her body leaning far out she reached her arms to them as they did to her; but the speed soon became too great, a few reckless enthusiasts still ran along, the rest remained behind in a cloud of steam, and lamented. Her handkerchief was still visible like a dove against a dark sky.

As she drew back she felt an aching void,

but she remembered her mother's eyes; had they the same look in them? Yes.

So she tried to appear as though she were not excited or agitated. She took her hat off and put it above her. But her mother's eyes had awakened the reaction which was latent in herself, conflicting feelings surged within her; she tried to conceal them, tried to recover herself, then threw herself down, turned her face away, and lay full length on the seat. A little while after, her mother heard her crying; she saw it too, from the heaving of her back.

Presently the daughter felt the mother's glove-less hand under her head. She was pushing a cushion underneath it. This did her good, merely to feel that her mother wanted her to sleep. Yes, she longed terribly to sleep. And in a few minutes she slept.

PART II

The river cut its way through the landscape in long curves. From the south bow window in the hotel, the mother and daughter followed its course through tangled underwood and birch forest ; sometimes it disappeared, and then shone out again, and at last became fully visible. There was a great deal of traffic going on, the hum of it reached their ears.

Down at the station, loaded trucks were being wheeled about. Behind the hotel were the works, the sawmill ; smothered thuds and blows were heard, and more faintly the roar of the waterfall ; over everything else the shrill sound of the planks as the saw went through them. This was one of the great timber districts ; the pine-trees darkened the heights as far as one could see, and that was very far, for the valley was broad and straight.

"Dear, it is nearly seven o'clock. What has become of the horses?"

"I had thought of sleeping here to-night, and not starting till to-morrow morning."

"Sleep here, mother?" She turned towards her mother with a look of surprise.

"I want very much to talk to you this evening."

The daughter recognised in her mother's eyes the same expression she had seen there at the station at Christiania: and she flushed. Then she turned back again into the room.

"Yes, suppose we take a walk." The mother came and put her arm round her neck.

Shortly after they were down by the river. It was between lights, and the softened hues of plain and ridge gave one a feeling of uncertainty.

A perfumed air was wafted from wood and meadow, and the rush of the river rose fiercely to their ears.

"It was of your father I wished to speak."

"My father?"

The daughter tried to stop her, but the mother went on.

"It was here I first saw him. Did you never hear his name mentioned in Christiania?"

" No." A tolerably long silence followed the " No."

" If I have never spoken of him freely, I had my reasons, Magne. You shall hear them now. For now I can tell you everything; I have not been able to do so before."

She waited for the daughter to make some rejoinder ; but she made none.

The mother turned half round and pointed up towards the station, that is, towards the house which stood beside it.

" Can you see that broad roof there, to the right of the hotel ? There are the assembly rooms, the library, and the rest. Your father has the credit of it; he gave all the timber. Well, it was there I first saw him, or rather from there I first saw him. I sat among the people who were going to hear him ; the whole of the ground-floor is one single room with broad sloping galleries, and it is built after the American fashion ; you know that your father went over there when he had finished his studies. Come, now, let us go on farther ; I love this path by the riverside. I walked along it with your father just six weeks to the hour and day after I had first seen him, and by that time we were married."

" I know."

" You also know that I was maid of honour to the Queen when I came here. She intended going farther out towards the fjord, but first we were to spend a few days here among the mountains.

" We came here one Saturday afternoon (as you and I have to-day) and remained over Sunday. There was a great crowd of people on Sunday to see the Queen; they knew she was to go to church. In the afternoon they all thronged to the assembly rooms to hear your father speak. I had seen the announcement of it in the hotel. The Queen read it too; I stood at her side and said, ' I do so terribly want to go.' ' Yes, go,' she answered, ' but you must be escorted by one of the gentlemen-in-waiting.' ' Here among the peasants ! ' I asked, and I took measures to go alone.

" I found a seat under the gallery, but near a large window, from which I could see a long way down the road. And as Karl Mander didn't come at the right time (he very seldom did) all

necks were stretched to get a glimpse of him on
the road; so I saw that he was to come from
that direction. I looked, too, with the rest, and
a long way off there were three men visible,
walking arm-in-arm, one tall and two smaller,
the tallest in the middle. I have very good
sight, and thought at once that he could not be
one of those, for they had been having too festive
a time. They happened to stand still just at the
moment, then they came along wavering, first to
the right, then to the left. People began to
whisper and titter. As the three drew nearer I
felt instinctively that the tall one was Karl
Mander, and felt ashamed."

"Was he drunk?"

"Yes, he was, and the others as well; and
very drunk too, both the doctor and the lawyer;
and the worst of it was, they were neither of
them his friends or partisans. It was a trick
they had played on him, for that was what people
were in the habit of doing. They had undertaken to make him drunk; but they had become
still more drunk themselves."

"How horrible, mother!" She wanted to stop;
but the mother went on.

"Yes. I had read all kinds of things about Karl Mander—but it was a different thing to see him."

"Were you not afraid?"

"Yes. It was disgusting. But when they came near enough for me to distinguish their faces, and all the people in the crowd who could see them laughed aloud, I shook off my fear; and when they came quite clóse, Karl Mander appeared to me such a marvel that I absolutely delighted in him. I admit it."

"How a marvel?"

"He was the embodiment of beaming joy! Picture a whole brigade of cavalry in the maddest gallop, you would not get such a sense of exuberant delight! The powerful figure with the mighty head held these two little men, one under each arm, as though he were dragging along two poachers. And as he did so he laughed and shouted like a boisterous child. He looked as kindly and gladsome as the longest day in the year up at the North Pole. As for the others who had set themselves to make him tipsy—for, as I have told you, it was the fashionable amusement at that time to make Karl Mander drunk—he brought them alongside in triumph. He was tremendously proud of it. He was tall and broad-shouldered, in his light checked woollen suit, which was very thin and fine ; for he could not endure heat, he was foremost among the worshippers of cold water, and bathed in it, even when he had to break the ice. He held his hat, which was a soft one and could be folded up, in his left hand. That was how he was always seen ; he never wore his hat at home, and out of doors he carried it in his hand.

"A great bushy head of hair, extraordinarily thick and brown ; which at this moment was falling over the lofty brow—(yes, your brow is like his)—and then the beard ! I have never seen so beautiful a beard. It was of a light colour and very thick, but the chief peculiarity of it was its delicate curliness. It was positively beautiful in itself—as a beard seldom is.

"And then those deep shining eyes—yours are *something* like them—and the clearly cut curve of the nose ! He was a gentleman."

"Was he ? "

"Heaven ! haven't I managed to give you that impression ? "

" Yes, yes—but others have———" She was silent, and the mother paused.

" Magne ! I have not been able, I have not wished, to shield you from all this. As long as you were a child, a young girl, I could not explain everything to you exactly as it was. It would also have led you to try to defend that which you had not yet the power to defend, and that would have done you harm. And there was something else besides.

" But now you shall know it. Since your childhood I have never given you any advice which did not come from your father. You never saw him, but all the same I can say that you have never seen nor heard anything but him. Through me, you understand ! "

" How so, mother ? "

" Well, we are coming to that. Now I must make you understand how I came to marry him."

" Yes, dear ! "

" He stood there on the platform and drank down water, glass after glass. He drank the entire contents of the water-bottle and called for more. The people laughed, and he laughed. He held the water-bottle and glass in a drunken grasp, and he looked up and round him, as though he was not properly conscious of himself or of us. And he laughed. But through it all I saw the godlike in him.

"A free man's open, joyous spirit, dear; unruffled self-reliance in reaching out for that which he needed. You should have seen his firm, capable hands, hardened by toil. And his face—the face of a man who overflows with all good gifts."

"What did people say?"

"They knew him, they were only amused. And he was amused. When he began to speak he had his tongue completely under control. It seemed to me that the voice was unnatural, it sounded as though it came from inward depths. But it was his natural voice. He had hardly begun when something happened. A crowd of ladies and gentlemen strolled by, among them some of the Queen's suite. We could see them from our place near the window, and he saw them too ; we saw that they pointed in.

"He stopped short, turned quite pale, and drew a breath so deep that we all heard it. Then he drank more water. It was long before he could go on speaking. They all looked at him, some whispered among themselves. Up to now he had spoken like a great machine which gives the first irregular beats with pauses between. But now he rose, and when he began to speak again he was sober. I tell you he was absolutely sober. Let me tell you by degrees, or you won't understand.

"His speech—do you know to what it can be compared ? A fugue of Bach's. There was something fulminating but abundant, uninterruptedly abundant, and often so gentle ; but there was this great difference, that he often groped for a word, changed it, altered it again, and yet it was incessant, and reverberant in spite of it all—that was the wonderful part of it. An irresistible reckless eagerness and haste. One wondered if there could be more, and there was always more, and nearly always something extraordinary.

"I had often heard people described as being possessed by some force of nature, but I had never seen it. Least of all at the Court, where marked personality is rare. I was at last face to face with one. The man who stood there:

was *obliged* to speak—in the same way, probably, as at a generous table he was *obliged* to drink. I knew that he managed his two farms, and worked on them himself when he had time, and I imagined that I could see the giant finding relaxation in the work ; but I saw clearly that his mind would work on as actively all the same, and that head and hands would vie with each other which should weary first.

"It was of work that he spoke. He led off by a reference to the Queen.

" ' Who is she ? ' he asked ; then he answered with some kindly feeling words about her. Then he asked again : ' Who is she ? ' He replied with another inquiry : ' Does she earn her own bread ? '

"This he held was the first obligation of all grown-up human beings who had the power to do it. That was the first standard we should apply to one another.

" ' Does she earn her own bread ? Do those who are in her suite earn theirs ? '

" ' No,' he answered, ' they don't earn it. They live on that which others have earned, and are earning.

" 'What do they do? Brain work? No, they live by the brain work of others. How do they spend their days then?

" 'In enjoyment, mental and bodily enjoyment of that which others have done and are doing. In luxury, in idleness, in social formalities, in king-worship, in travelling, in repose do they live.' At this point he kept on substituting one word for another, but made no pause.

"Their greatest exertion, he said, was to try to enjoy an additional party or an extra levee, their greatest danger was a cold or an overtaxed digestion.

"And in order that the fruit of other people's labour should not be taken from them, what did they do?

"They opposed everything which threatened them with a new order of things. They opposed all needful changes. They opposed emancipation for those who had nothing in the world. They behaved as though society had from eternity been ordained for them, as though they could say 'Thus far and no farther.'

"You will understand that I have learnt all these ideas from my intercourse with him. I could after my own fashion make all his speeches, and that more fluently; but I believe that this exchanging one word for another, and his perpetually halting over it, made the words that he finally did choose more significant. For my part, I have written down everything that happened in our short life together."

" Everything ? "

"I mean everything that mattered at all. Everything, everything. He never wrote a line, he said he had no time, he despised it. And when death took him from me and from us all, what had I better to do ? No—don't interrupt me—let me go on telling you ! He repeated the same thought from the religious point of view. It was his way to look at the same idea from every side. He said that to-day he had been to see an old woman who said that she couldn't go to church because she had no shoes. There was no end of trouble to get her some, for the two shoe-shops wouldn't sell any on Sunday, but she got them. He saw her afterwards go to church, just at the same time as the Queen and her suite.

" And he thought, there are so many who sit

in church with wretched shoes on, and so many
at home, who dare not venture to church because
of their miserable shoes, or the rest of their
miserable garments. Who are they who have
such wretched shoes and clothing ? They who
have worked most, worked until they are broken
with toil.

"But those who have not worked have ten
pairs of shoes, they could have a thousand;
and clothes too, in the greatest superfluity.
He had not been to church, he said, but he
knew that there they held forth as though it
were the most natural thing in the world that
those who had shoes should give them to those
who had none. You would gather from the
preaching that Jesus Himself had taught it,
Jesus had come to make all men happy, and
this was the best way! For it is written, 'He
went about doing good.'

"But they all went home from church just
as they came; and no exchange of shoes took
place, nor exchange of clothing either. One
went back to his superfluity of leisure, the
other to his poverty and want, and those who
had not been able to go at all, because they

were too poor, remained after the service as they had been before it.

"Such, you see, is our Christianity, he said. And *he* had a right to speak, I can tell you, because he shared his 'superfluity' with others."

"But still you live in a certain comfort ? "

"Yes, in his opinion every one had a right to do so. The man who recognised that he was called on to sacrifice his comfort also should do it ; but for most educated people comfort was the indispensable condition of work and help the foundation of happiness. And there was a charm of beauty about it, too, which is a rare incentive.

"No, what he demanded was that all those who could should support themselves—hear that, my daughter !—and that those who had superfluity should employ it in work which should be fruitful for others. He called that Church cowardly and shameless which did not make that demand without respect of persons."

"Like Tolstoi, then ? "

"No, they were very different. Tolstoi is a Slav by birth, Ivan the Terrible and Tolstoi both of them ; for these contradictions presuppose each other. The one did everything by force, the other resists nothing. The one had to crush all wills under his own in order to make room for himself, the other will willingly yield, knowing that a desire, once satisfied, dies. The Slav impulse towards tyranny, the Slav impulse towards martyrdom, the same passionate excess in both. Born of the same people, and under the same conditions.

" All the freedom *we* in Western Europe enjoy we have attained by keeping bounds, not for ourselves alone but for others. And also by resisting. It is weakness that knows no limits : strength ordains limits and observes them."

" But yet the Bible teaches——"

" Yes, yes, but the Bible is from the East too ; the Westerns act *in opposition to* the Bible. What I am saying comes from your father."

" Did he know Tolstoï ? "

" No, but what I have been saying is older than either the Bible or Tolstoï."

" Then he was a great orator ? "

" That I could hardly venture to call him ; he could not be reckoned among the prophets, but among the seers.

" Now don't interrupt me. He believed that in another hundred years to live in idleness and superfluity would be looked upon by most people as now we look upon a life of fraud and crime."

" Oh, mother, how did you feel about it ? "

" His voice seemed to surge and vibrate in my ears both day and night. A storm-cloud seemed to surround me. Not as though he thundered or commanded. No, it was his personality, and something in the voice itself. It was deep and restrained, as though from a cavern ; it came fitfully, but without cessation. I believe he spoke for over two hours. Whomever he happened to look at looked at him, and if he looked away the other continued to gaze—he couldn't help it, you understand. His eyes blazed with inward fire, he stood bending forward like a tree on a hill-side. The image of the forest rose in my mind. Later, when I was nearer to him, the breath of the forest seemed to hang round him. And his skin was so clear ! For instance, that part of his throat which was not sunburnt, because he stooped. When he lifted his head, you can't imagine how pure and fair it was.

" Ah, how have I drifted into this train of

thought ? But never mind, I have drifted into it—
and I will follow it out—it takes me to your father's
side again ! O Magne, how I loved him ! how I
shall always love him !" She burst into tears—
the girl's heart beat against hers. The softened
colours of wood and plain in the uncertain light,
the strenuous roar of the river seemed to sunder
them from each other ; the surroundings were at
war with their mood ; but the more closely did
they cling together, each supporting the other.

"Magne, you mustn't ask me to put what
I have to say to you in any sort of order. I
only know the point I am aiming at.

"Yes, he was like the nature that surrounded
him, fashioned on a generous scale and rich with
hidden treasures: so much I dimly grasped.
Everything I saw was new to me, the face of
nature as well as the rest. I had travelled, but
not in Norway.

"It is said of us women that we are not able
to analyse those whom we love, but only worship
them in the abstract. But he had a friend, his
best friend ; he could analyse him ; the poet. He
was present at Karl Mander's last meeting, and
he came to me from it when your father was

dead. We talked together of everything as much as I then could. He wrote about him the most beautiful things that have ever been written. I know them by heart ; I know everything by heart that has been worthily written about your father."

" Do you know what it was he wrote ? "

" ' If the landscape I see around me could speak like a human being ; if the dark lofty ridge could find speech to answer the river, and those two began to talk across the underwood, then you would know the impression made when Karl Mander had spoken so long that the vibration of his deep voice and the thoughts it uttered had melted into one.

" ' Halting and with difficulty, as though from inward depths clumsily fumbling for words, he always arrived at the same goal. The thought was at last as clear and lucid as a birch leaf held against the sunlight.' "

" Was it then——"

"No, don't interrupt me ! ' Karl Mander often seemed to me as unlike all other people as though he belonged to a different order of things. He was not like an individual, he represented a race. He swept by like a mighty river : at the mercy of chance and natural obstacles, perhaps, but ever rolling on. So was he, both in life and in speech. Neither was his voice merely individual, it had in it the reverberation of a torrent—a melancholy, captivating harmony, but monotonous, unceasing.'"

"That surely is what the sea sounds like. mother?"

The mother was as much carried away by her memories as animated in her movements, as eager in her glance as a young girl. Now she stopped.

" Like the sea, do you say ? No, no, no, not like the sea. The sea is only an eye. No, dear, not like the sea; there were warm depths and hiding-places in his nature such as the sea has not. One had a sense of intimate security and comfort with him. He was capable of the most self-forgetting devotion. Listen further. ' Karl Mander was chosen,' he wrote, ' chosen as a fore-runner before the people's own time should come —chosen because he was good and blameless; his message to futurity was not soiled in his soul.'"

" That is beautiful."

" Child, can you imagine how I was carried

away? I had had a vague feeling that the surroundings of my life were unreal; here was something that was real.

"And he himself! We women do not love that which is lofty merely because it is lofty; no, there must be a certain weakness too—something that appeals to our help; we must feel a mission. And you cannot conceive how powerful and yet powerless he was."

" How powerless, mother ? "

" Well, when he came—in that condition——"

" Yes, of course."

" And his way of expressing himself. He never found the right words first, he stopped and changed them even as they poured out. And, in the meantime, if he caught something up in his hand he stood there with it. If it were the tumbler—and it generally was—he grasped it tightly, and so, because of it, would keep his hand still for a quarter of an hour at a time. His personality was so pathetically simple, or how shall I express it ? He was a seer, not a prophet—yes, I told you that before. But seers are quite different, they don't know themselves so well, they have absolutely no vanity. Heavens, how I longed to go and take off his cuffs! One could see that he was not accustomed to wear them : some one must have told him that it would not do to make a speech from a platform without cuffs on. He had crumpled and tumbled them ; they had come unfastened, or perhaps never had been fastened ; they got in the way and slipped over his hands. He struggled with them. There was something wrong about the waistcoat too ; it was buttoned wrong, I believe, and puckered up at one side, so that it showed one of his braces— to me at any rate, where I sat looking at him sideways and with the light full upon him. Ah, that mighty creature with the stooping head! The tears rose in my eyes. Who would not have been willing to follow him ?

"I felt as deeply as it could be felt that *he must be helped.* I did not know that I was to help him ; I only knew that he must be helped and sustained."

A rush of memory so overpowered her that she could not go on, she turned away.

PART III

THE daughter saw her mother in a new light. Surely this was not she who ordered and managed her house, who sent wise letters to her, with earnest, well-weighed words! How her passion had transfigured and beautified her!

"But how did you feel, dearest mother?"

"I was not conscious of what I felt. We went away from there the day after, and our next halting-place was close to his two farms. I had my wits so far about me, however, that when some of us had to be quartered out, I chose the house which was nearest his. And when the tempest within me was no longer to be resisted I wrote to him, without signing my name. I asked him for an interview. He was to meet me on the road that went through his wood, between his house and ours. I dropped the letter into his own letter-box on the road. You can imagine what a state I was in when I tell you that I had appointed ten o'clock in the evening, as I thought that then it would be dark ! I had not noticed that it was still light at that time, so far north had we come. The result was that I did not dare to go out until eleven, and then I was sure there would be no one to meet. But there he was ! Mighty and stooping, his hat pressed together in his hand, he came forward, hesitatingly, shyly, and awkwardly, glad. ' I knew it was you,' he said."

" Oh, mother ! what did you do ? "

" All at once I began to wonder where I had got the courage from ! I did not even know what I wanted with him ! When I saw him I could have turned and fled. But his wonderful gait, those long firm strides, his hat in hand, his shaggy head. . . . I felt I must see it all. And the wonderful thing he said : ' I knew it was you.' How could he have known it ? I don't remember whether I asked him, or if he saw my surprise, but he explained that he had seen me as we came away from the lecture ; he had heard who I was. It was wonderful to hear the deep voice, which for me meant something so absolutely exceptional, as though resounding from

the far future, making embarrassed excuses for
having said anything that might have wounded
me. Before he succeeded in getting out 'wounded
you,' he stammered—'wounded the Queen—
wounded the Queen and her ladies—wounded
you !' He had so many other subjects he might
have touched upon, and so many other themes
he might have chosen. He could have said so
much that was good of the Queen, much that he
knew to be true ; but he had forgotten it. So
he went on, his eyes looking into mine—trust-
ing, but commanding eyes, whose attraction I
felt. There seemed to be an echo in the silent
wood of his unfathomable honesty. And his
eyes went on repeating, 'Don't you believe it,
too ?' No one can imagine how unconscious he
was of the effect they produced. He spoke, and I
listened, and we drew nearer and nearer to each
other. But the joy I felt, and which could not
find words—what should I have said ? At last
it became uncontrollable—it burst all bounds.
I suddenly heard myself laugh ! And you should
have seen how, all of a sudden, he laughed with
me ! Laughed, so that the woods re-echoed !
The fishermen were just rowing past to be at

their post when the sun should rise. They rested on their oars and listened. They all knew the sound of his laughter. I recognised its sound from the time when I saw him coming between his two satellites. There was a faun in him—a northern faun, of course, a wild man of the woods, unrestrained, but innocent, leading two bears, one under each arm! Yes, something of that kind. Not a troll, you understand, for they are stupid and malignant."

"You say 'innocent,' mother? How do you mean that he was innocent, since he was so wild?"

"Because nothing harmed him. Whatever he might have known or experienced, he remained a great child all the same. Yes, I tell you, refined and as aloof from evil. He had such a power of refinement in himself that what did not appeal to his nature was annihilated by it. It no longer existed for him."

"Oh, mother, how was it all? Oh, why have you been given this experience, and not I!" She had hardly spoken the words when she turned and ran swiftly away. The mother let her alone; she sat on a stone and waited her return. It was good to rest with her thoughts.

She sat a long time alone, and would willingly have sat longer; but the clouds began to gather. Then Magne came back with a nosegay of the most beautiful wild flowers and delicate grasses arranged about a fir branch covered with cones, grey-green young cones.

"Mother, he was like this nosegay, wasn't he? What, dear mother, are you crying?"

"I am crying for joy, my child; for joy and regret both together. One day you will come to understand that those are the most comforting tears in the world."

But Magne had thrown herself down on the ground by her side. "Mother, you don't know how happy you have made me to-day!"

"I see I have, dear child; I was right to wait; it was a struggle, but I did right."

"Mother, dear mother, let us go back to the forest at home, to the road through our forest! Let me hear more! It was there it happened, then! Mother, tell me! What came next, sweetest mother! Ah, how lovely you are! There is always something fresh to discover in you."

The mother stroked her hair in silence, soothingly.

"Mother, I know that woodland road on summer nights. Laura walked there with me when she was engaged, and told me how it all happened, and the fishers rode past that time too, just as we came to an opening. We hid ourselves behind a great boulder; and the thrush began to sing, and many other birds, but the thing that affected me most was the scented air."

"Yes, doesn't it? And that is why I have always thought since that the woodland scent hung around Karl. Ah, I must tell you how curiously unconscious he was—what other word can I use? We stood still and looked over the lake. 'Oh, what a longing that gives,' said I. 'Yes, a longing to bathe, doesn't it?' said he."

Magne broke into hearty laughter; the mother smiled. "Now it no longer seems so strange to me. The water was more to him than it is to us—he used to plunge into a bath at the most unexpected times: when he was not to be found in his farms or at his office, that was always where he was. It was his strongest natural craving; he loved the cold embrace of the elements, he said.

"And how he laughed to himself when he saw how I was laughing! We laughed in unison."

"Then, mother, what happened? I can really wait no longer."

"I came home just as other people were getting up. And the next night was like that one, and the next after that, and the next after that again. One night it rained, and we both walked along under the same umbrella, and that was what brought things to a climax."

"To a climax?—how?

"After once being obliged to walk arm-in-arm, we always went arm-in-arm afterwards."

"But other people, mother? Weren't you afraid of what they would say?"

"No; other people didn't exist for me. I can't remember how it all went on—it happened that one night we had sat down."

"Ah! now we are coming to it!"

"I asked to be allowed to sit down; I felt I could walk no longer. The night was glorious—silence and we two! He went on talking with his eyes looking into mine; he didn't know himself how they shone with happiness. I couldn't speak—I could hardly breathe—I was obliged to rest. And a few minutes after I sat on his knee."

"Was it he who———"

"I cannot quite remember. I only remember the first time my arms were about his neck and my face against his hair and beard. It was rapture, something absolutely new—it was bliss. The feeling of those giant arms round me transported me far, far away. But we were there on the boulder all the same."

"Were you as though beside yourself———?"

"Yes, that is just it! that is what it is called —but it really means being in possession of oneself, raised up to higher things. By his side I was myself twice over. That is love; nothing else deserves the name."

"Mother, mother! it was you, then, who sprang into his arms! It was you!"

"Yes, I am afraid it was I. I suppose he was too modest, too shy to begin that sort of thing. Yes, I know in my heart it was I. For life must be preserved. It was a question of nothing less. To be able to help him, to follow him, and worship him, and give myself up to him, that or nothing. I believe, too, that

that was what I said to him, if I did say a single word."

"Oh, you know that you said it!"

"I believe I did; but in looking back upon such moments as those one does not know whether one was feeling or speaking." She looked out into the long valley. She stood like one who is about to sing, with lifted head and open mouth, listening for the music before it sounds. But it was not so: it was the sound of bygone music that she heard.

A little while afterwards she said quite softly —the daughter was obliged to draw nearer to her, for the sound of the river swallowed up some of the words:

"Now you shall hear something, Magne; you have never heard it from me, and others are not likely to have told you."

"What is it, mother? You almost frighten me."

"At the time I met your father I was already engaged."

"What do you say? You, mother?"

"Yes, I was engaged, and was to be married; and it was my last month with the Queen.

The engagement had taken place, and was to be carried out with the highest sanction."

" But to whom ? "

" Ah, that is it ! Didn't I tell you before, that at the time I met your father I was in absolute despair ? "

" You, mother ? No."

" I did not believe that life had anything to offer, or that I had anything to wait for. Most girls who arrive at the age of twenty-eight without anything having happened to them, anything that is worth rousing themselves for, believe that nothing is worth caring about. The age, or about that age, is the most perilous."

" How do you mean ? "

" That is when most girls come to despair."

She took her daughter's arm, which she pressed, and so they walked on together.

" I must confess it all to you "—but there she stopped.

" Who was it, mother ? " She said it so softly that her mother didn't hear, but she knew what it was.

" It was some one for whom you have but small respect, my child. And you are right."

" My uncle ? "

" How did that occur to you ? "

" I don't know.　But was it he ? "

" Yes, it was.　Yes, I see you don't understand it.　I never understood it myself, either.
Think of your father, and of him !　And just
about the same time, too.　What do you think
of me ?　But, oh ! take care of yourself, my child."

" Mother ? "

" Well, well—*you* have a mother, and I had
none.　And I was at Court, and, as I told you,
at the perilous age when nothing seems worth
caring about any longer.　Of course I, too, had
been playing the same game that I have been
looking on at to-day, but not with your aptitude.
Yes, you may turn away your face.　I had come
to feel a certain disgust with life—for myself
among the rest—and so I went on refusing people
till it was too late in the day."

" But—with my uncle ! "　Magne broke out
again.

" We looked upon him differently at that time.
But I don't want to go into all that again now.
I will only admit that it was horrible.　So you
may think what you like about it—I mean as to
how it came about."

The daughter took her arm away and looked at her mother.

" Yes, Magne, we don't always do as we mean to do, and I have told you I was at the perilous age. And so you can understand how I felt when I saw your father—there was something more than pettiness and frivolity in me after all."

" But the others, mother ! How could you put it in the proper light to the others, to the Court, to our relations, to my uncle, and all his people ? Surely there must have been a fuss and a scandal that you had to hold up your head against ? "

" Wait, Magne, we will let all that alone till later. There were no ' others ' at all ! Some fishermen had seen us, and they had taken measures to find out who I was. Before it was known I had gone away, and within one month I was his wife. I had fallen into the hands of a man who did things thoroughly and at once. He was too simple to conceive any other way than to go straight forward. So it took place without any obstacles."

" And what did people say ? Was it a good thing for my father—I mean in people's opinion —that he had married you ? "

"You mean that he should marry a maid of honour?" she smiled. "Do you know what people said of it? Why, Karl Mander had publicly maligned the Queen—one of her maids of honour had heard him, and a month after she had eloped with him. That was about it. She had chosen the roughest man in the country. That was what people said."

"Naturally."

"A year after a tourist wrote in a newspaper that he had seen the runaway maid of honour standing at the washing-tub. Ha, ha! It was true enough for that matter. You had come, then, and it was harvest-time, and I was obliged to lend a hand. We both did."

"Mother, mother, what was he like at home? When you were together, I mean? Wasn't it perfect? It must have been the greatest and best thing the world had to give? Mother, mother, all my life I must be grateful to you for having treasured this up for me till now, for before I should not have understood it."

"Yes, isn't it so? Such things cannot be told to a child, nor to a half-grown girl. But I am not telling you, now, only for the sake of telling you. You ask how things were when we were together. Picture him to yourself first. An unselfish, devoted nature that was very little understood, by some few perhaps, in a way, but even by them not adequately. The result was that when he believed he had found sympathy, he poured himself out so unrestrainedly that people laughed at him. If he were in company he drank, or rather was made to drink, until he was tipsy, and so let his untamable nature take the bit in its teeth. Do you know—yes, I must tell you this. At a party a lady (she is now married to the captain here) set to work to draw him out for the amusement of the others. She was very bright and witty ; she appeared to be entirely carried away by him, so that she could not listen to him enough, could not question him enough, and all the while poured more and more wine into his glass. She drank with him ; she made all the others drink with him."

" Good heavens, mother ! "

" Do you know where it all ended ? In the cowhouse. They locked him into the cowhouse by himself. His frenzy of rage brought on a nervous attack.   She it was whom he saw from the window as he stood on the platform that day. It was then he became sober."

The mother and daughter walked on in silence.

" You knew nothing of all this at that time, did you, mother ?—not until later ? "

" No ; if I had known it, I believe I should have gone straight up to him, taken him by the hand, and greeted him with all my heart."

" I should too, mother ! "

" Since my life with him I have thought a great deal.   Do you know, I believe geniuses have this characteristic of confiding impulsiveness, and therefore the people and conditions that surround them are of all the greater importance. But most important of all is it that they should have a woman's help.   And, according to the nature of that help, so things go with them. Karl Mander had got into the habit of speaking in monologues.   He got on best among peasants. They disturbed him least.   Books, meditations, farming, bathing, and now and then an orgie, a speech, or, for preference, one on top of the other—that had been his life up to then."

" But he didn't drink, mother ?   There was no need for him to drink, was there ? "

" No more need than for you or for me.   It
was simply an outburst of mere high spirits, or
repressed longing for happiness.   So the last
time———".

"Yes, that time! Oh, why were you not there?".

" You had come to us then, my child, and I
could not ; I was nursing you at my breast.
The whole thing would have gone off happily, if
some one at the banquet after the meeting had
not been so imprudent as to propose my health !
Then he let himself go !   There was the theme of
themes, and he had never unbosomed himself
about it to any one !   The toast applied the
match to his inward fire ; his exultant joy blazed
up.   He made a speech in praise of at least
twenty of my characteristics, of marriage, of
fatherhood.   He———"

She could not go on.   She sat down, her
daughter by her ; they were both in tears.   The
roar of the river swept pitilessly past them, and
yet it seemed to bring them a kind of comfort.
All the tears we may shed avail nothing.   It
goes on its way, and nothing arrests its determined course to the sea.

Through the voice of nature the whispers of
memory brought back his tragic end.   It came

over them both again how, after the banquet, he
wanted to refresh himself with a bath. How
every one tried to dissuade him, but it was no
use. How he sprang in from a great height,
took longer and longer strokes out, as though
each one of them were taking him home, was
seized by cramp and sank.

"Mother, there is so much I still want to
hear about your life together?" Then, after a
moment: "Mother, you must give me that too!
Yes, you have told me so much, so very much
about it. But not just the thing I want to know
now! The love, mother, the devotion between
you both! Mother, that must have been something too wonderful to realise."

"Beyond all comprehension, my child!
Beyond all understanding! And, do you know,
the calumnies that were spread about us,
especially the miserable anonymous letters, all
kinds of meanness, it all helped. For each time
we found in each other a perfect refuge. He
was not so thin-skinned in such matters as I.
It was through me that he first came to understand them—how to manage the petty incidents
of social life. The leaders of society in this

little country are not of pure Norwegian race,
but of foreign descent. A man like him could
never learn to keep pace with them. But I was
one of them, and, through the effect on me, he
understood ! When he once was started on a
line of thought you can't imagine how fast he
went. He was a discoverer, an investigator by
nature. But when he first rightly found out
what I had exposed myself to by choosing him,
ah ! how the thought of it spurred him on ! If
ever any one has been rewarded here on the
earth, he rewarded me. Night and day, the
whole summer, the whole autumn, the whole
winter, the whole spring, we were never apart.
Our life was one continued flight from the outer
world, but it was a flight into Paradise. He
refused all invitations ; he had hardly time to
speak to the people who came to see him ; he
would not have them in the house. He and I,
and I and he, in the big rooms, and the smaller
ones, he in mine or I in his. And on the
country roads, in the fields, in the mountain
pastures, on the lake, on the ice, working,
superintending together, together always, or if
we were away from each other it was but to

meet again at the very earliest moment. But the more we were together the more I came to understand the wealth of his nature. What impressed me most about him was not the flow of ideas, it was the man himself. To fathom his perfect uprightness, clear to the very bottom, gave me the most glorious moments I have known. His devotion to me—or what shall I call it ?—was all summed up in one image—his mighty head on my lap ! There he often rested it, and always said, ' How good it is to be here !' "

And the daughter laid her head in her mother's lap and sobbed.

It began to rain. They rose and went home again. The little assembly house up by the station loomed more indistinct but more inviting through the rain. And the landscape took on a greater harmony of tints and greater friendliness ; the scent from the birch-trees seemed trebled.

" Yes, my child. I believe I have given you some of his aspirations. Have I not ? She bent down towards her face.

Instead of answering, the daughter pressed closer to her.

They waited a moment before going on.

"You have a longing, yearning nature ; you inherited it, and I have stimulated it in you by what I learnt from him. I have put great objects, noble men and women before you. So did he ; I have plunged you into lofty thoughts, as he plunged in nature to refresh his own. I knew when I sent you away from me that I was acting in accordance with his spirit. But I knew best with what armour you were equipped : it came to you from him. And yet . . . . Magne ! "

The daughter instinctively drew her arm from within the mother's and stood still. She needed to rest on her own strength, as it were.

"Yes, I see it ; that is the third time to-day. You feel that I am taking hold upon you ; and I *will* take hold upon you. It was at the party at your uncle's that you said to me, when I was going in to supper, ' Mother, you might as well keep on your gloves.' You were ashamed of my work-hardened hands."

"Mother, mother !" The daughter covered her face and turned away.

"I will tell you this, my child, that without these work-hardened hands you would not be what you are now ; if you have lived in a society where it is considered shameful for a woman to have such hands, you have lived in an evil society. And to-day you enjoyed that society, enjoyed it as though you believed you yourself had attained a certain greatness in it."

" No, mother ; no, no ! "

" Yes, you did ! You may perhaps have felt a pang of conscience or of fear ; that may be, for I was there. But now the moment has come for you to choose ; I wanted your choice to be made before you should cross the threshold of your father's house, my child. Work—or else the other thing."

" Oh, mother, you wrong me ! If only you knew ! "

" If I can make you love your father—and I shall do all I can, and you have capacity—if I can make you really, rightly love him, then I know all that you will be able to do. We women must love in order to have faith."

Printed by BALLANTYNE, HANSON & Co.
London & Edinburgh

The Pioneer Series.

12mo, cloth, 3s. net; or, paper covers, 2s. 6d. net.

The Athenæum.—"If this series keeps up to the present high level of interest, novel readers will have fresh cause for gratitude to Mr. Heinemann."

The Daily Telegraph.—"Mr. Heinemann's genial nursery of up-to-date romance."

The Observer.—"The smart Pioneer Series."

The Manchester Courier.—"The Pioneer Series promises to be as original as many other of Mr. Heinemann's ventures."

JOANNA TRAILL, SPINSTER. By ANNIE E. HOLDSWORTH.

GEORGE MANDEVILLE'S HUSBAND. By C. E. RAIMOND.

THE WINGS OF ICARUS. By LAURENCE ALMA TADEMA.

THE GREEN CARNATION. By R. S. HICHENS.

AN ALTAR OF EARTH. By THYMOL MONK.

A STREET IN SUBURBIA. By E. W. PUGH.

THE NEW MOON. By C. E. RAIMOND.

MILLY'S STORY. By Mrs. MONTAGUE CRACKANTHORPE.

MRS. MUSGRAVE—AND HER HUSBAND. By RICHARD MARSH.

THE DEMAGOGUE AND LADY PHAYRE. By WILLIAM J. LOCKE.

THE RED BADGE OF COURAGE. By STEPHEN CRANE.

HER OWN DEVICES. By C. G. COMPTON.

PAPIER MACHÉ. By CHARLES ALLEN.

THE NEW VIRTUE. By Mrs. OSCAR BERINGER.

ACROSS AN ULSTER BOG. By M. HAMILTON.

ONE OF GOD'S DILEMMAS. By ALLEN UPWARD.

Other Volumes to follow.

Heinemann's International Library.

Edited by EDMUND GOSSE. Price 3*s.* 6*d.* cloth, 2*s.* 6*d.* paper.

*** Each Volume has an Introduction specially written by the Editor.

Times.—"A venture which deserves encouragement."

IN GOD'S WAY. From the Norwegian of BJÖRNSTJERNE BJÖRNSON.

PIERRE AND JEAN. From the French of GUY DE MAUPASSANT.

THE CHIEF JUSTICE. From the German of KARL EMIL FRANZOS, Author of "For the Right," &c.

WORK WHILE YE HAVE THE LIGHT. From the Russian of COUNT TOLSTOY.

FANTASY. From the Italian of MATILDE SERAO.

FROTH. From the Spanish of DON ARMANDO PALACIO VALDÉS.

FOOTSTEPS OF FATE. From the Dutch of LOUIS COUPERUS.

PEPITA JIMÉNEZ. From the Spanish of JUAN VALERA.

THE COMMODORE'S DAUGHTERS. From the Norwegian of JONAS LIE.

THE HERITAGE OF THE KURTS. From the Norwegian of BJÖRNSTJERNE BJÖRNSON.

LOU. From the German of BARON VON ROBERTS.

DOÑA LUZ. From the Spanish of JUAN VALERA.

THE JEW. From the Polish of JOSEPH IGNATIUS KRASZEWSKI.

UNDER THE YOKE. From the Bulgarian of IVAN VAZOFF.

FAREWELL LOVE! From the Italian of MATILDE SERAO.

THE GRANDEE. From the Spanish of DON ARMANDO PALACIO VALDÉS.

A COMMON STORY. From the Russian of GONTCHAROFF.

WOMAN'S FOLLY. From the Italian of GEMMA FERRUGGIA.

SIREN VOICES. From the Danish of J. G. JACOBSEN.

Popular 3s. 6d. Novels.

ELI'S DAUGHTER. By J. H. Pearce, Author of "Inconsequent Lives."

INCONSEQUENT LIVES. A Village Chronicle. By J. H. Pearce, Author of "Esther Pentreath," &c.

HER OWN FOLK. (En Famille). By Hector Malot, Author of "No Relations." Translated by Lady Mary Loyd.

AVENGED ON SOCIETY. By H. F. Wood.

A COMEDY OF MASKS. By Ernest Dowson and Arthur Moore.

THE JUSTIFICATION OF ANDREW LEBRUN. By F. Barrett.

A CONSPIRACY OF SILENCE. By G. Colmore.

A DAUGHTER OF MUSIC. By G. Colmore.

CAPT'N DAVY'S HONEYMOON. The Blind Mother, and The Last Confession. By Hall Caine.

THE RETURN OF THE O'MAHONY. By Harold Frederic. With Illustrations.

IN THE VALLEY. By Harold Frederic. With Illustrations.

THE COPPERHEAD, and other Stories of the North during the American War. By Harold Frederic.

KITTY'S FATHER. By Frank Barrett.

A QUESTION OF TASTE. By Maarten Maartens.

COME LIVE WITH ME AND BE MY LOVE. By Robert Buchanan.

A ROMANCE OF THE CAPE FRONTIER. By Bertram Mitford.

'TWEEN SNOW AND FIRE. A Tale of the Kafir War of 1877. By Bertram Mitford.

popular 3s. 6d. Novels.

APPASSIONATA: A Musician's Story. By ELSA D'ESTERRE-KEELING.

ACCORDING TO ST. JOHN. By AMÉLIE RIVES.

ORIOLE'S DAUGHTER. By JESSIE FOTHER-GILL.

THE MASTER OF THE MAGICIANS. By ELIZABETH STUART PHELPS and HERBERT D. WARD.

THE HEAD OF THE FIRM. By Mrs. RIDDELL.

THE STORY OF A PENITENT SOUL. By ADELINE SERGEANT.

THE SURRENDER OF MARGARET BELLARMINE. By ADELINE SERGEANT.

THE TOWER OF TADDEO. By OUIDA.

THE O'CONNORS OF BALLINAHINCH. By Mrs. HUNGERFORD.

NOR WIFE, NOR MAID. By Mrs. HUNGERFORD.

THE HOYDEN. By Mrs. HUNGERFORD.

MAMMON. A Novel. By Mrs. ALEXANDER.

DAUGHTERS OF MEN. By HANNAH LYNCH.

A LITTLE MINX. By ADA CAMBRIDGE.

A MARKED MAN : Some Episodes in his Life. By ADA CAMBRIDGE.

THE THREE MISS KINGS. By ADA CAMBRIDGE.

NOT ALL IN VAIN. By ADA CAMBRIDGE.

A KNIGHT OF THE WHITE FEATHER. By TASMA.

UNCLE PIPER OF PIPER'S HILL. By TASMA.

THE PENANCE OF PORTIA JAMES. By TASMA.

Six Shilling Novels.

THE HEAVENLY TWINS. By SARAH GRAND.

IDEALA. By SARAH GRAND.

OUR MANIFOLD NATURE. By SARAH GRAND. With Portrait of the Author.

A SUPERFLUOUS WOMAN.

TRANSITION. By the Author of "A Superfluous Woman."

THE STORY OF A MODERN WOMAN. By ELLA HEPWORTH DIXON.

THE LAST SENTENCE. By MAXWELL GRAY.

THE POTTER'S THUMB. By F. A. STEEL.

FROM THE FIVE RIVERS. By FLORA ANNIE STEEL.

RELICS. By FRANCES MACNAB.

THE MASTER. By I. ZANGWILL.

THE KING OF SCHNORRERS. By I. ZANGWILL. With over Ninety Illustrations.

CHILDREN OF THE GHETTO. By I. ZANGWILL.

THE PREMIER AND THE PAINTER. A Fantastic Romance. By I. ZANGWILL and LOUIS COWEN.

THE EBB-TIDE. By ROBERT LOUIS STEVENSON and LLOYD OSBOURNE.

THE MANXMAN. By HALL CAINE.

THE BONDMAN. A New Saga. By HALL CAINE.

THE SCAPEGOAT. By HALL CAINE.

Six Shilling Novels.

ELDER CONKLIN; and other Stories. By FRANK HARRIS.

THE RECIPE FOR DIAMONDS. By C. J. CUTLIFFE HYNE.

THE COUNTESS RADNA. By W. E. NORRIS.

A VICTIM OF GOOD LUCK. By W. E. NORRIS.

THE DANCER IN YELLOW. By W. E. NORRIS.

THE NAULAHKA. A Tale of West and East. By RUDYARD KIPLING and WOLCOTT BALESTIER.

A PASTORAL PLAYED OUT. By MARY L. PENDERED.

CHIMÆRA. By F. MABEL ROBINSON.

MISS GRACE OF ALL SOULS'. By W. TIREBUCK.

AT THE GATE OF SAMARIA. By W. J. LOCKE.

A DAUGHTER OF THIS WORLD. By F. BATTERSHALL.

THE FOLLY OF EUSTACE. By ROBERT HICHENS.

AN IMAGINATIVE MAN. By ROBERT HICHENS.

THE ELEVENTH COMMANDMENT. By HALLIWELL SUTCLIFFE.

ILLUMINATION. By HAROLD FREDERIC.

HERBERT VANLENNERT. By C. F. KEARY.

CORRUPTION. By PERCY WHITE.

MR. BAILEY MARTIN. By PERCY WHITE.

Six Shilling Novels.

A SELF-DENYING ORDINANCE. By M. HAMILTON.

A COMEDY OF SENTIMENT. By MAX NORDAU.

THE MALADY OF THE CENTURY. By MAX NORDAU.

THE ISLAND OF DR. MOREAU. By H. G. WELLS.

STORIES FOR NINON. By ÉMILE ZOLA. With a portrait by Will Rothenstein.

THE YEARS THAT THE LOCUST HATH EATEN. By ANNIE E. HOLDSWORTH.

IN HASTE AND AT LEISURE. By Mrs. LYNN LINTON. Author of "Joshua Davidson," &c.

A DRAMA IN DUTCH. By Z. Z.

THE WORLD AND A MAN. By Z. Z.

BENEFITS FORGOT. By WOLCOTT BALESTIER.

SENTIMENTAL STUDIES. By HUBERT CRACKANTHORPE.

WITHOUT SIN. By MARTIN J. PRITCHARD.

TERMINATIONS. By HENRY JAMES.

EMBARRASSMENTS. By HENRY JAMES.

OUT OF DUE SEASON. By ADELINE SERGEANT.

THE FAILURE OF SIBYL FLETCHER. By ADELINE SERGEANT.

www.ingramcontent.com/pod-product-compliance
Lightning Source LLC
Chambersburg PA
CBHW020107030726
47498CB00006B/1995